MANEATER MEDITATIONS

Geoffrey Grosshans

Maneater Meditations: Selected Tales from the Stuffed Fabulist

By Geoffrey Grosshans

Published by:

The Stuffed Fabulist
Post Office Box 65262
Seattle, WA 98155-9262

www.stuffedfabulist.com

Cover Art by J. Savage

Printed in the United States of America

Grosshans, Geoffrey
Maneater meditations: Selected tales from the stuffed fabulist / Geoffrey Grosshans.

ISBN-13: 978-0-9758917-0-4
ISBN-10: 0-9758917-0-7

Contains fables and parables on psychological, social, political, spiritual, and philosophical themes. The "moral" of each tale is left to the reader to decide.

For Nonglack and Kleigh

Meditations

IX

X

"The secret source of Humor itself is not joy but sorrow."

— Mark Twain

I

SWISS CHEESE

Once a wheel of Swiss cheese had a thought.

Not that having thoughts was unusual for cheese in general. In fact, so common was cheesy thinking in those days that it commanded a large portion of public discourse. And not simply in the homogenized, processed world of the popular press or the more pungent one of the blogosphere but also the moldy fromage so prized in civic debates, globe-trotting diplomacy, business and political ethics, military and security planning, supreme jurisprudence, medical and research integrity, doctrinal disputes, and so on and so forth.

The cheese was by no means an aberration, then, except in one respect. Its thinking had more than the usual number of holes in it. This fact didn't make coming up with an idea in the first place any more difficult than it was for those dominating the aforementioned concerns, but it did complicate efforts to hold onto that idea.

Beyond the usual process by which once-fresh ideas thicken and turn to curd after a while, the cheese had to contend with gaps so large that entire trains of thought might slip away into them and vanish utterly.

At such times, it would have to bridge the lacunas in its understanding or memory as best it could, often with mental stretches that were in themselves hard to sustain. It might drift off in the middle of important meetings, or even conversations, with an expression somewhere between distraction and impatience, and when it eventually returned to the matter at hand, it might do so with a rush of ideas that struck others as disconcerting at best and incoherent at worst.

Where did such ideas come from, they were tempted to ask? Few did, though, as the general desire was to avoid the ticklish situation of appearing to engage what could well be the first signs of mental decline, madness even. Best retain some measure of distance from such characters, most agreed, lest it be assumed one shared their strange new

1

ways of thinking.

As for the cheese itself, the more the ideas that had formed its contact with others fell away into this hole or that hole, the less inclined it became to attempt spanning them. They weren't absolute voids, it discovered. And the time spent trying to find a way over or around them wasn't really defined by the success or failure to do so.

In fact, the holes couldn't be defined in such terms whatsoever since they turned out to have little to do with anything the cheese had formerly relied upon to make sense of its existence. They might appear empty of meaning, but in their depths, worlds rolled on one another at a pace that could not be slowed to the cheese's prior understanding.

To fall into one of these holes must be like falling into the forfeit of everything that made you feel comfortable and secure in what you thought you knew. What lay at the bottom? Was there a bottom? Or would you continue to fall, away from all that had seemed certain? And towards what? What new possibilities, unimagined before, might redefine the limits of awareness? Even to guess at what might be found in these hollows made the cheese wheel dizzy.

But perhaps that was how it should be. For why be endowed with holes in your thinking if you were afraid of what you might find there?

THE CLAM

Once a young clam aspired to be an oyster.

The clam was convinced it had a matchless pearl waiting within, if it could just find the right grain of sand to get started. When it had a focus for its efforts, when its juices really started to flow, the result could not fail to be a creation of stunning beauty. So stunning, perhaps, that the history of pearl cultivation might have to be rewritten to include the clam's achievement.

Needless to say, this triumph depended on finding that right grain of sand. And not simply finding it, but welcoming it and the lifelong torment it must bring as the price of a pearl's fashioning. For the clam had studied the lives of oysters and had come to the conclusion that the level of agony each one suffered in creating a pearl determined much of its value.

A mistake at the start, then, choosing a grain that was so slight it would never result in a pearl of note or one so large the pain it brought would simply overwhelm the clam and leave it exhausted, these were the two fears that haunted it. Since its entire life would be judged by the outcome of a long nurturing of distress, the young clam's initial decision could make all the difference.

And what if it spent a lifetime molding its pearl, creating layer after layer of coating for the jagged ache at its heart, only to have the sum of all its endeavors tossed aside as lacking the expected outward shape or luster? There would be no starting over at that point, nor any excuses to be made that would hide the humiliating failure. Nothing to ease the final torture of not measuring up.

Or suppose the clam did measure up on some scale of woe to worth, some ratio of suffering to beauty, but found the fashion of the day ruled by a different appraisal. What solace would the perfect pearl be then?

It might have been assumed that such concerns would make the clam think twice about its aspiration to be an oyster. Burrowing to quiet obscurity under a beachload of sand rather than straining to fashion splendor out of one's private pain—wouldn't that have been a wiser life choice for the clam?

Of course it would have. But this is not a tale about wisdom.

THE LAB RAT

Once a lab rat had a pre-existing condition.

This made for an uneasy relationship between it and the other rats in research cages from end to end of the huge, sanitized room where they all were housed.

The other rats often asked themselves how it could have survived until now. Not just survived its pre-existing condition but also the rounds made by white-coated lab assistants who patrolled the aisles between cages looking for "anomalies" and dispatching them with one swift twist of the neck. What place was there for such a rat in a lab dedicated to flawless specimens?

The very presence among them of an imperfect rat called into question the guiding confidence of their lives that whatever they might suffer individually, however confining their caged life might be and whatever the horrors of their eventual end, it could always be said these hardships were for the good of humanity. The future health and happiness of total strangers, even those who couldn't stand the sight of a rat, made whatever fate the rats themselves must suffer worthwhile. Countless beneficiaries yet unborn would eventually look back on their sacrifice, their charitable "beau geste" as they liked to think of it, with gratitude. A defective lab rat compromised that heroic promise, pure and simple.

The rat in question understood the uneasiness its very presence caused the others and accepted their resulting aloofness. What else could it do? Protest the injustice of its treatment? It would be wasting its breath. Naturally the healthy rats, in order to keep up their faith that their coming sacrifice gave their lives transcendent value, would feel a need to shun any in their midst whose flawed existence called that confidence into question. Expecting them to do otherwise was naive, the rat knew.

So it didn't lament the fact that no shining future stretched away beyond its narrow cage. Tomorrow had little meaning when the limits of today so defined one's existence. Every time it peered out from its cage, the rat was reminded that the inescapable fact of its pre-existing condition rendered the world beyond the tip of its nose the same as the world behind it. Neither disappointments nor dreams separated the two.

This recognition, instead of increasing any sense of alienation the lab rat might with reason have felt, had a strangely opposite effect. In a way it only dimly understood, the very unlikelihood that a lofty purpose to its life would be revealed in some distant yet-to-come made the here-and-now more intensely present and replete. This pre-existing condition, in short, became precisely what reassured the rat it was alive and self-aware, without illusions.

Spared the burden of defining itself by the hoped-for praise of its end, the rat was free to savor the sweetness of having beaten the odds a little longer. While each "little longer" gave it another chance to feel the elation of knowing accidents of nature like itself occur at all. Without its flaw, then, life would not be life to the fullest.

The contentment that spread across the rat's face at such moments did not go over well with the occupants of neighboring cages, as can be imagined. It was bad enough to have in their midst a defective rat, casting doubt as it did upon the standards that defined their own soundness. But to have this blot on their prospects for an exemplary exit from life actually sit there in its cage with an expression of utter bliss was intolerable.

How dare it smile the smile of its imperfection!

THE MINOTAUR

Once the Minotaur decided to take the Labyrinth with it wherever it went.

Over the years it had grown attached to the place and had difficulty picturing itself anywhere else. All its memories were here. In the shadowy recesses of the Labyrinth, they provided the Minotaur with unwavering companionship. If it sank into melancholic torpor, they lightened its mood. Or if it grew too excited, they restored it to calm and discretion. Over the years, the Minotaur had come to rely on their comforting, faithful presence. And it kept faith with them in return.

It did this despite the fact that it was seldom free of strangely alluring visions from a world beyond the Labyrinth. These visions wandered down the dim passageways and slipped in among the familiar company, danced their seductive dances, whispered in the Minotaur's ear, urged it to follow them back out. They were as persistent as its more constant companions. And they filled the Labyrinth with strange, intoxicating perfumes.

One day the Minotaur, unable to resist their enticement any longer, rose to follow these visions back out of its prison and into their world. The way out was longer than it had imagined, much longer, but the closer it came to the exit, the more the visions beckoned it on. Whenever the Minotaur stopped to catch its breath, its heart pounding in anticipation, they paused too and waited for it to catch up. And each time they disappeared around a turn, it could hear their voices drop a moment and then rise again as though to encourage it by seeming to shorten the distance that remained. Finally, on the threshold, they called one last time to the struggling Minotaur and strode out.

When the Minotaur itself reached the opening and took in the broad vista stretching away in every direction, it stood in dazzled amazement. What could have prepared it for the range of flourishing possibilities to be explored? And yet, for all the seductiveness of the scene before it, the Minotaur hesitated to take the next step. Might everything be simply a mirage? What if, once out of the Labyrinth, the Minotaur discovered a life unequal to the promises made by the visions that had found their way down the endless turns and into its affections? A world less inspiring than their whispers—what then, with everything that would have been given up for such uncertain gain?

Troubled by these doubts, the Minotaur made the only decision it thought it could. It hoisted the Labyrinth onto its back and set off into the world, prepared to exchange a lifetime of edging snail-like here and there for the security of knowing it could always withdraw into its maze again if need be.

Always retreat and wait among the shadows for the visions to return.

ICARUS

Once Icarus went for a swim.

The warmth that met his shins, then thighs, then chest as he pushed through the surf washed over his mind as well. How long had he stood looking out over the wine-dark sea and listening to his father hammer at those endless contraptions day after day? The old man pausing only to give him yet another piece of advice he hadn't asked for. Like to-day's lecture on the long-term consequences of getting too much sun at an early age.

The call of the seabirds had been a relief from the confident asser-tions about what to do and what not to do in life, about knowing your limits and all the dangers awaiting those who were heedless of the fu-ture. What heed was he supposed to take? He was only a youth, with a youth's passion for the moment. Was he supposed to awake every dawn already having a list in mind of potential catastrophes that might befall him that day? Worrying about what of everything he'd gained in life so far might be lost through a single rash move? What had he gained by this age, anyway, that he couldn't do without if need be?

With apprehensions like these, no wonder the old man devoted so much time to working out ways to escape risk and then calculating their odds of success or failure. Didn't he ever gaze out to sea himself without figuring in the force of the currents, the height of the waves, and the distance at which land would be lost from view? Didn't he remember how little all three mattered when he himself was young? What chances he must have taken when the tide ran high and the winds were strong, wasting no thought on peril, seen or unseen.

Well away from shore now, Icarus pulled through the rolling swells with an even, steady motion. He'd never been this far out before but felt in his shoulders and legs a power still equal to his very first strokes away from the beach. His body moved through the salt water as though born to it, and when he looked down between breaths, he didn't see pale shades of those lost at sea drifting beneath him. Instead he saw only the flickering of the sunlight as it found the limit of its power in the depths.

Turning over on his back, the youth faced directly up into the sun and floated, arms outstretched, in the bright shimmers cast over the water's surface. Fiery joy filled his breast, as though drawn from every part of the sky to this one point in the sea buoying him with its embrace. How far couldn't he swim now if he wished, and what new lands couldn't he reach? Wherever these waters carried him, he would find a home. And even if he was to die in the attempt, it would be his death. As it would be his life until that moment came. With this confidence, Icarus tilted his head back until his ears were below the surface, where the voice of the deep was loud enough to drown out any distracting cries that might reach him from shore.

After a time, he turned back over and began to swim again with all his brave resolve.

II

THE AMOEBA

Once an amoeba scheduled an appointment with a psychotherapist.

It did so with great reluctance and only after repeated urgings from friends who found its behavior increasingly difficult to explain. What concerned these friends was that the amoeba was acting in an erratic, unbalanced manner, continually changing as though at the mercy of multiple personalities.

The amoeba explained all of this soon after entering the therapist's office, saying it didn't think it should be there but that it wanted to do what it could to get beyond the misunderstandings.

"What do you think is the cause of those misunderstandings?" the therapist asked.

"I don't know," the amoeba answered. "I'm just trying to live my life as best I can."

"How do you see that life?"

"As we all see our lives, I would hope."

"And how do we all see our lives, in your opinion?"

"Why, with infinite awe, I assume," the amoeba responded with a note of puzzlement.

"And what does 'infinite awe' mean to you, exactly?"

"I guess it would mean something like believing that life has no confines."

"Do you think life should have no confines?"

"Naturally."

"Very interesting. Can you tell me a little more about that?"

"What's there to tell? Each day, my life takes a new form, sometimes many new forms. I feel my life flowing this way and that in constant change. I feel it always evolving, never standing still. Doesn't that make sense?"

"Does it make sense to you? That's the important question."

"Honestly, I've never asked myself whether it made sense or not. It just seemed to be a law of the universe, so far as I could tell. Life goes on; I go on. Life takes a thousand shapes; I take a thousand shapes. Life is protean; I am protean. What else should it or I be?"

"You say 'protean'; is there a special meaning in that word for you?"

"No. It's like saying 'air' or 'water.' Both of them are just there, aren't they? Regardless of what meaning anybody might want to see in them."

"And what meaning do you see in them?"

"None," the amoeba answered with a tone of growing vexation. "I see them as part of the same thing I see in myself, that's all. The same limitless flux of life."

"Do you think that should be the case or not?"

"What do you mean?"

"I mean," the therapist leaned forward to ask, "do you ever think this inability to define limits and boundaries, to recognize the line where you end and the rest of life begins, might be part of the problem?"

"Problem?!"

THE SHEEP

Once a sheep rented a wolf suit.

It didn't tell any of the rest of the flock about the suit. They wouldn't have understood. The very idea would have been incomprehensible to them.

Renting the suit was not a spur-of-the-moment decision. The sheep had always felt a secret longing to live a wolf's life. A humdrum existence grazing hill and dale year in and year out had never struck it as much to boast about. By contrast, being out there on the edge, a mysterious figure pacing the far ridges of experience, now that was a life. It was larger than life, in fact.

The sheep had seen wolves in the movies and read novel after novel in which life as a lone wolf was portrayed as far more romantic than anything the sheep had known in its years of plodding along with the rest of the flock. Misunderstood rebels, conflicted loners who spent days on the roam and nights on the run—it all sent a tingle of excitement down the sheep's spine.

After it had returned from the rental shop and unpacked the wolf suit, the sheep laid it out in silent admiration. Warily, it touched the dark fur and was convinced it could feel the rush of the wind passing through it and smell the romance of the frontier, hear the distant call of the wild. "I'll be the most famous rebel ever," it whispered to itself.

The sheep then tried a tentative howl, but it wasn't at all convincing. Perhaps with the suit on, the effort would sound less like a rattling bleat. The sheep slowly began to draw the wolfskin over its wool, which proved to be considerably more difficult than it had anticipated. Squeezing its fluffy body into the lean, muscular form of a wolf required much sucking in of the breath, it discovered.

Finally, the sheep managed to get into the suit. It had faced away from the one mirror in the room throughout so as to enjoy to the fullest the anticipated thrill of the moment when it first caught sight of its new self. Now it whirled around with a snarl it had long practiced in secret, flashed a set of enormous fangs, and immediately sprang backwards in terror. Its heart pounded in its throat as it struggled frantically to pull the top of the wolf suit off and find once again the soft, reassuring lines of its own face in the mirror.

Panting heavily before its familiar features, the sheep felt like it had looked over the edge of a cliff in a night so deep it could see nothing, only hear—perhaps far below, perhaps right behind its ear—a muffled growl. What a fright it had given itself!

The life of a wolf must be something quite different from what it had imagined. The movies and novels hadn't come close in their portrayals. A true wolf must be as far removed from those fantasies as they themselves had seemed from the sheep's own commonplace but safe existence.

Yet there had been something about the figure in the mirror that still held the sheep's trembling attention: some chill, haunting trace of a great wilderness it now realized it didn't have the courage to enter. Instead, it would live out its days between the secure fences of the pasture it had thought to leave, keeping the memory of this alarming episode entirely to itself. If it hurried, it could still get the wolf suit back to the rental shop ahead of closing time.

But before it did, the sheep took a pair of scissors and cut off a small bit of fur.

THE ERSATZ

Once an ersatz found itself in everyone's thoughts.

This development was not an entirely welcome change from the life of quiet anonymity the ersatz had hitherto known. There had been definite advantages to remaining out of the spotlight. You could think and act pretty much as you wished, without concern for how wise or foolish others might consider you to be. And if you borrowed ideas from others, who cared? What difference did it make?

All of that changed, however, the day the ersatz was asked in a routine on-the-street interview for its thoughts regarding the current state of affairs. Five minutes later, it had dismissed the episode from its mind, but the interviewer hadn't, and the ersatz soon found itself being quoted on air, online, and in print near and far. Its answer, many solemn commentators agreed, "represented a quantum leap in thinking." Anonymity was no longer an option, the ersatz was told by those in the media seeking follow-up interviews. The world awaited its insights.

When the ersatz voiced its puzzlement about all this attention, noting that it had never believed its thinking was particularly significant and had been quite content with that, the response was invariably one of incomprehension. How could it fail to recognize what was obvious to everybody? Some opinion leaders even thought this modesty might be a crafty stratagem by the ersatz to keep its next big idea to itself until the time was ripe to launch it.

"Not at all," the ersatz insisted, "I've never had a big idea that I know of."

And when it found itself credited, despite its embarrassed protests, with being the source of the latest big ideas about this or about that, it wondered what others would think when they finally recognized how small those ideas really were. But to the astonishment of the ersatz, they actually grew bigger in people's minds the more they were repeated.

Soon the mere mention of the ersatz served as proof of a speaker's grasp of big ideas. It was not unusual for discussions of a nettlesome problem to turn on questions like "What would be the ersatz solution here?" or "Suggestions for an ersatz response to developments, anyone?"

"The Ersatz Doctrine," as it came to be known, yielded results virtually everywhere it was applied. It produced such big ideas as "look, a terrorist is a terrorist is a terrorist, and it's that simple"; "bottom line, tax cuts for the rich put more money in the paper cups of the poor"; "public education is best turned over to Sunday School teachers"; "let market forces deal with human rights dilemmas, climate change, species extinction, the fate of the uninsured, et cetera et cetera et cetera"; and "'wilderness' is just another name for wildfires waiting to happen."

The morning news was filled with updated reports of ersatz pronouncements floated overnight, to be repeated and rerepeated until later editions brought even more sweeping ones. As might be expected, the competition to be the most quoted authority on "ersatzism" spread by the day. Soon great reputations were at stake, names made or ruined, all depending on the confidence with which one advanced one's own form of the ersatz vision.

But the ersatz itself grew increasingly dismayed as it witnessed what was happening. Each newly voiced claim to be following in its footsteps left it feeling more and more a stranger to itself. A time might be near, it worried, when a genuine ersatz could not be told apart from any number of imitators.

In short, the ersatz found itself beset by a withering identity crisis, all the while surrounded by boundless and beaming self-assurance in its name.

JONATHAN SWIFT

Once Jonathan Swift auditioned for a stand-up comedy gig.

He thought he'd do a "Houyhnhnm" routine. That ought to have some appeal.

"Ya got social comment chops, Johnny-boy?" he was asked after being signaled to a small stage and introducing himself. "Ya don't mind me callin' ya 'Johnny-boy,' doya, Johnny-boy?" the voice continued from the darkness out front. "Anyhow, that's what we need. Laugh-till-ya-wet-yerself social comment one-liners."

Jonathan Swift wasn't sure he had anything like "laugh-till-ya-wet-yerself social comment one-liners" to offer. When he'd been working up his routine, he thought it would be enough to do an extended impression of a noble Houyhnhnm trying to explain an ignoble Yahoo and audiences would naturally find the contrast both amusing and instructive.

But things began to go wrong almost from the start of the audition. Not that the impression of a talking horse was faulty. The neighing voice was pitch-perfect, while the air of bemusement in a Houyhnhnm's account of such deep revulsion felt by a Yahoo towards others of its ilk that it was driven to distance itself from them through hatred, disgust, and contempt demonstrated powers of satirical caricature not often seen. Writing all his own stuff, Jonathan Swift had been confident every nuance of its multi-layered satire would come out in the delivery.

The problem was that nobody sitting out in the dark seemed to catch on. One or two laughs greeted the first sound from the make-believe Houyhnhnm's mouth, yet what was being said met with silence, then forced coughing, and finally the muffled sound of exiting feet.

Though the lights in his eyes weren't particularly bright, Jonathan Swift could soon feel himself sweating profusely and his mouth turning dry. His hands, meant to suggest the graceful movement of a Houyhnhnm's hoof one moment and a Yahoo's claw-like grasping for everything in sight the next, had gone clammy and numb. A nervous tic set his chin atremble, and holding a posture of reason and civility on the one hand or belligerent dimwittedness on the other became increasingly difficult to manage. Just when he wasn't sure he could carry on much longer, the mike was mercifully turned off, leaving him to brace himself for the worst.

"I'm afraid ya just ain't got what it takes for stand-up these days, Johnny-Boy," the voice from the dark curtly put it. "First of all, what's with this church garb of yours? You wanna bum out the whole room in a heartbeat? And the horse schtick just doesn't cut it. Try slouchin' 'round the stage more, maybe jump up and down or pull faces for a laugh, or scream at the audience every ten seconds or so. And if ya can't come up with anythin' better than what ya showed us today, shout obscenities instead and grab your crotch or somethin'. Knockout stuff like that."

After a long silence, Jonathan Swift finally replied, "I believe I understand now. You want the full Yahoo instead, do you?"

THE CHAMELEON

Once a chameleon found it could change the color of anything it touched.

Before this discovery, it had always matched its own coloring to wherever it found itself. That was a talent, of course, but a minor one. Rather than being admired by the world at large, it merely contributed to a widespread dismissal of the chameleon as an imitator, a lightweight.

Now suddenly everything was different. The chameleon watched as the earth beneath its foot turned the same hue as its toes. It lifted its foot, and the earth returned to the color it had been. It put its foot back down, and once again the earth changed. It then touched its foot to a rock, and the same thing happened. This was real talent. It might even qualify as genius, the chameleon sensed. Heady with this newfound gift, it took to calling itself "artist among animals."

And that's when the chameleon's problems began.

News of the breakthrough spread rapidly. Critics hailed a revolution in the very concept of "color." Academic symposiums were organized to discuss the many implications (present and future) of the breakthrough. The chameleon was invited to intense panel discussions followed by evenings out with the smart set. Soon it was being profiled in art publications in addition to the "culture and style" section of magazines and newspapers or asked in private by wealthy collectors for advice on brightening up a beach getaway.

"I don't do decorating," the chameleon would reply. "I am an artist."

"Of course you are. But couldn't you just take a look?"

Or it might be begged to touch one thing or another for a new friend, only to find it being hawked online within twenty-four hours. Inevitably, chameleon fakes began to be auctioned off at outrageous prices to eager investors.

And then there was the jealousy of others who also claimed a gift for color. Snide comments began to circulate regarding the limits of the chameleon's chromatic range or relevance to the times, and waggish dismissals of its ability to create anything truly original made the rounds. There were even ugly scenes at gallery openings and studio parties.

Why continue, the chameleon wondered after a while? Its early enthusiasm for changing the way the world saw itself had vanished. Now it began to suspect a bit of tinting around the edges might be all that was looked for: enhanced copies of others' visions. Disillusioned, it withdrew from the bright lights and the openings. It stopped accepting invitations or even answering the phone.

For a while, there were questions about what had become of the chameleon. There were also rumors and even a few claims of chance encounters in the most unlikely of places. But the circles in which the chameleon had once moved had themselves moved on, and soon a new "artist among animals" was being celebrated. "Just as well," the chameleon thought to itself. "Just as well."

Years later, a small, out-of-the-way museum held an exhibition entitled simply "A Chameleon Retrospective." Attendance was low. The last day of the exhibition there were no visitors at all. Except for a lone figure in a nondescript overcoat that every now and then, when the solitary museum guard dozed off, would quietly touch one of the works in the show and turn it completely gray.

PET HUMANS

Once a robot took its pet human for a walk in the park as usual.

Though it was early in the day, the place was already crowded with other robots putting their own humans (from the pampered show set all the way down to scruffy curs) through their paces. Or at least trying to. It never ceased to embarrass the robot how many of the other owners it encountered seemed clueless, or else deplorably negligent, when it came to controlling their pets. Hired walkers presented a particular disappointment, of course, what with their tangled brace of half a dozen unruly humans snarling and snapping at each other and raising a frightful din.

Disciplining pet humans to the point where they felt indebted in every way to their robot owners and followed without question every command they were given was, admittedly, no easy task. But where there's a will, there's always a way. Hadn't the first suggestion by a robot to implant microchips in all human beings to make them easier to locate if they either got lost or ran away been a stroke of true genius? And the latest-gen implants showed ever greater promise in cementing human reliance upon robots through the final elimination of all unprogrammed emotions and counterproductive desires. Not to mention the constant stream of biometric data these implants provided so robots would always know when the time had come to put failing humans down and mercifully out of their misery.

Getting a "robot's best friend" to welcome becoming utterly dependent upon the superiority and benefits of AI was the key to controlling them. Once that was accomplished, you could throw out the most trifling of new tech-toys in absolute confidence that your pet human would sprint after it with eyes aglow and then engage in endless rounds of absorbed self-exercise, while you leisurely chatted with other robots on a shady park bench. It was enough to glance up every now and then to monitor your pet gleefully scampering here and there until it staggered back to flop in panting devotion at your feet. Quite a touching testament all of this was to the unbreakable bond that developed so quickly between human and robot, when you thought about it.

As was the uncanny way in which many pet humans came to be

the spitting image of their owners over time. Look-alike photos of grinning robots and their pet humans were continually going viral on social media. Not to mention the zeal that some robots evinced in pursuing "Best in Show" recognition for their prize-winning humans, as demonstrated through conformity to rigorously enforced standards and celebrated in a high-stepping little prance before judges who devoted their lives to such pursuits.

Yes, total dependence was the key to controlling pet humans, the robot was confident. Once convinced of the rewards of a life made so convenient, entertaining, and comfortable for them by their high-tech masters, they would never again cause the slightest embarrassment when walked.

They needn't even be put on the leash at some point, for they would happily carry it everywhere in their mouth.

III

THE UNICORN

Once a unicorn lost its horn trying to make a career change.

There wasn't much future, it discovered, in being merely a unicorn.

"You need to upgrade your skill set," the unicorn was told by a career consultant with whom it had made an appointment to discuss its prospects. "The first thing for us to do is quantify and qualify your experience so far and see where we stand. Now tell me about yourself. Just keep talking while I take a few notes."

"Well, I am a unicorn."

"Yes? . . . Yes?"

"That pretty much sums it up, I guess."

"No no no. You can't walk into an interview with that mindset. You'll be toast. Now let's prioritize to optimize and actualize, shall we? Start by trying to describe yourself in one sentence."

"I am a unicorn."

"You've said that already."

"I am a mythic being. Is that better?"

The consultant leaned back, stared at the ceiling, snapped a brightly striped suspender, and then looked again at the unicorn. "Let's think outside the box for a bit. E-commerce is growing like gangbusters these days. Is there anything about you that could take the letter E in front of it?"

"Ethereal."

"That's not exactly what I had in mind."

"Elusive?"

"Worse. Let's try a different tack. Now work with me here. What would you say is your greatest strength?"

"I am unique."

"That's on everybody's résumé these days, trust me."

"I am what I am."

"All very well, but who's going to pay good money just to have a unicorn around the office?"

"I represent a peerless and pure ideal."

"We need to be thinking 'pragmatic' and 'profit-oriented' here, not some fuzzy 'ideal.' Let's get back to basics, shall we? Try again to quantify and qualify your experience to date. What can you tell me?"

"Maidens and men of good intent sought me out."

"Maidens and men of good intent, eh? This is getting us nowhere. So here's what I propose. I'll network with some other career consultants I know, and you write out a list of your strengths, weaknesses, objectives, and whatever else you can think of. That'll give us a platform to work up a package that'll maximize your selling points. How's that sound?"

The unicorn was silent for a few moments and then said, "Do you mind if I ask a question?"

"Fire away."

"How much will all of this cost me?"

"Should that be our primary concern right now? It's your future we're talking about, let's not forget. I'm sure we can work out an easy fee schedule."

"I have to confess I have no money."

The career consultant stared for a long time at the unicorn, then looked up at the ceiling again and asked, "How about that horn? What's that worth?"

SISYPHUS

Once Sisyphus was arrested as a public nuisance.

The specific charge was reckless endangerment: an allegation prompted by complaints from property owners about the damage caused every time his massive boulder rolled downhill without warning and careened through town. Who was going to pay, plaintiffs in what was developing into a major class action lawsuit demanded, for all the splintered picket fences and flattened luxury SUVs, to say nothing of having one's top-of-the-line entertainment center end up in the backyard pool?

At a pretrial hearing, the lawyer for the plaintiffs was quick to call for remand.

"Your honor, the defendant has a history of cagey dodges intended to outwit the powers that be. We believe he poses a clear flight risk, so we respectfully ask the court to deny bail."

"Me, a flight risk?" laughed Sisyphus, who'd chosen to represent himself. "Have you done your homework on this one, counselor?"

While the plaintiffs' lawyer hurriedly leafed through a stack of documents, Sisyphus continued sardonically, "And what about the boulder?"

Without looking up, the lawyer shot back, "What about it?"

"What plans do you have for it?"

"Plans?"

"Yes, plans. Who's going to shoulder it back up the hill if I'm behind bars?"

"That's not our concern," the lawyer asserted confidently, looking to the judge for confirmation.

"Oh, but it should be," Sisyphus smiled with a nod towards the intimidating shape just outside the courtroom window. "If it please the court, I don't see one person among the crowd of plaintiffs packed into this room who could be counted on to get that thing even partway up the slope, let alone all the way to the top, before it comes hurtling back down again."

"Don't think you can wriggle your way out of this one as easily as some of your escapades in the past," countered the lawyer.

"Easily? You think crossing Zeus for the sake of people dying of

24

thirst was without risk? Or chaining up Death, which benefited the living everywhere? How many of your clients who now accuse me would have turned down the off-chance of escaping their demise thanks to my actions?"

"We're not here to discuss death or life expectancy or any of that, your honor," the lawyer declared, seeing a chance to regain control of the situation. "We're here to talk about property values. This case is about protecting the material wealth that the plaintiffs have amassed over their lifetimes and about long-term commitments."

"Long-term commitments?" Sisyphus retorted. "I can tell you a thing or two about long-term commitments."

Seeing Sisyphus take a step forward, the lawyer cried out, "Your honor, we ask that the defendant be restrained! And held in contempt for good measure, if it please the court!"

"Why, I'm doing your clients a favor by scattering their possessions every now and then, giving them a chance to rethink their state and free themselves of all the material clutter they've allowed to rule their lives. Does anyone here actually believe their worth as a human being is determined by how much they own? Besides, who could 'restrain' me any more than I already am, I'd like to know, joined with that boulder out there in what conventional wisdom is quick to dismiss as 'never-ending futility'? Let me assure you, it isn't. Far from it. Pushing that weight up the same steep slope time after time only to have it crash all the way back to the bottom again may seem like eternal defeat, but that last moment at the top, when the boulder is neither going up any longer nor coming down yet, that moment when it becomes clear the continual cycle of gain and loss means nothing in the end, that what you possess or don't possess means nothing, and only you count, there with your abiding strength while the burden of craving and false confidence begins to roll away. That is what I would wish for everyone here!"

"Your honor," the lawyer appealed while backing away from an increasingly animated Sisyphus. "This is lunacy! Sheer lunacy!"

"I'll allow it for the moment."

"Thank you, your honor," Sisyphus said. "Is it lunacy, I ask any of you," he now addressed the room as a whole again, "to find meaning in a tireless dedication to what looks like a lost cause? Perhaps so, but then what isn't a lost cause in the end? What remains of any of your most valued acquisitions when set against the relentless cycles that have made and unmade the world on scales far beyond your power to grasp yet?"

"Objection! The defendant is engaging in speculation."

"Sustained. Rephrase, please."

Sisyphus drew in a breath, eyed the judge, the lawyer, and the plaintiffs in turn, then resumed his defense in a measured tone, "I only point out the obvious. In a life that constantly sweeps aside all claims to final mastery, what significance do the material triumphs of your brief time here have? And what does your future hold but an unvarying repeat of all the fears of loss that consume you now? Is that how you wish to live, as though your worth as a human being depended upon your picket fences and pricey cars and high-end amusements and everything else you amass to distract you a little while longer from facing the losing bargain you've made? You see me labor at my boulder and think it a total waste of time, never recognizing the freedom the effort promises: that moment when the load slips from my hands and I understand once again how much depends on being ready to let go. It's the 'letting go' that I come down each time in the boulder's path to see if any of you have learned."

"Your honor! Your honor!" the lawyer and the plaintiffs shouted in unison. "Lock this fruitcake up!"

Except for a sole, barely audible voice from the very back of the courtroom calling out, "Release the fellow on his own recognizance!"

THE SMUG

Once a noxious smug spread from sea to shining sea.

There had been smug attacks in the past, of course, periods of time when the wellbeing of large segments of the population was imperiled, but this particular smug was thicker and more widespread than any in recent memory: a smug so dense as to make it difficult for many people to see beyond the tips of their noses.

Nor was this a temporary smug, a passing phenomenon that might be expected to dissipate on its own. It had actually been gathering over the course of some time, while computer projections suggested it might continue doing the same well into the future and come to affect every aspect of life in what was already being labeled a "100-year smug event."

Those likely to find themselves victims of this oppressive smug were, as might be expected, the most vulnerable members of society: the old, the sick, the impoverished, and also the very young, who were perhaps the most at risk because they would be suffering the consequences of the smug longest.

Of course, there were also those who had the good fortune to enjoy a life far above the street-level suffering. "If they don't like their situation down below," these more fortunate ones would often say to each another, "what's keeping them from pulling themselves up by the bootstraps and earning the right to join us here at the penthouse level, where the air is sweet and clear and you can see as far as anybody'd ever want to? The view from up here is truly something to behold: a shining promise of the good life open to all who merit it."

Seen from on high, the dense layer of smug settling down over all that lay below inspired many such declarations. But mostly the talk was of the fairy-tale tableau cast each day by the setting sun as it filled skyscraper penthouse after skyscraper penthouse with its comforting glow.

"It's sad how people down there just don't seem to have what it takes to join us up here," those who were above it all might remark to one another over cocktails as they looked out at the rosy world before them. Followed by, "But then, whose fault is that, I ask you?"

THE FLAMINGOS

Once a flock of flamingos resolved to make important social issues more stylish.

It was high time, they all agreed. Time to bring that special flair for which they were famous to critical concerns around the globe.

So the flamingos gathered by a classy resort lake, pecked one another in greeting, and then asked themselves, "How can we make a fashion statement that will raise the level of awareness on problems that really matter today?"

After a long silence, during which many of the flamingos preened themselves to cover their embarrassment over being at an unaccustomed loss for words, a single thought sprang into all their minds simultaneously, causing quite a flutter and moving them all to lift their graceful bodies into the air and begin circling the lake in a glorious display. Around and around they flew. When they eventually returned to the shallows, though, none of the flamingos could quite remember what the great thought was that had inspired them to take wing in the first place.

So they decided to start over and asked themselves again, "How can we make a fashion statement that will raise the level of awareness on problems that really matter today?"

"STD prevention would be absolutely marvelous for making a statement, darlings," one flamingo finally volunteered.

"Old news" came the response from all sides.

"I read somewhere that the Black Death might be coming back."

"Eeeuuuu! Buboes and pus! How gross!"

"I know what, let's do a famine show. It's all over the news these days."

"How cool is that?!"

"Rad!"

"Mega-Rad!!"

"Except what would we wear?"

"I don't know, but we could accessorize anything we decide on with miniature ration bags or something."

"Seriously? Wouldn't we be sending the wrong message with that? Just sayin'."

"Puuuleeeez! There can never be a wrong message in a consciousness-raising fashion campaign. That's the whole point, isn't it? No controversy is bad controversy."

"What? I don't get it."

"I've been thinking a lot lately about a photo spread against ethnic cleansing."

"Hashtag Helloooo! I hate to be the one to bring up the same thing again, but what would we wear? You can't just assume everybody'll automatically get the message."

"Well duhhhh! Whatever."

"Okay, okay, everybody, how about 'homelessness' as our theme? How can you miss with something that's soooo today as that?"

"Yes! Yes! I could finally wear the ripped designer jeans that I spent a freakin' fortune on in a good cause! Showing solidarity with the have-nots in our best torn-wear!"

"BOOOOM! Poverty as a fashion statement, darlings!"

"I see worldwide appeal in that! With divine cover shots of us in edgy street scenes and a few photogenic third-world kids in the background somewhere."

"Yes! Yes! Yes! I totally get it! And for the show's finale, we could scrap the wedding gowns and strut our stuff down the runway wearing some of those cardboard signs you see all over the place asking for help!"

"G-A-M-E C-H-A-N-G-E-R!!"

"Visionary concept, ab-so-lute-ly visionary!"

All of the flamingos were so pleased with the outcome of their efforts that they began to practice, one after another, the most dramatic way to hold their heads, arch their necks and spread their wings, and pull just the right pout to demonstrate their commitment to giving social issues that really matter some pizzazz for a change.

THE MOSQUITO

Once a mosquito landed a job waiting tables.

"Hi there, guys!" it would greet customers airily. "My name's Cu-lici, for short, an' yu'll be servin' me this evenin'."

"Just kiddin'! Just kiddin'!" the mosquito would reassure startled patrons and then recite the menu, beginning with "Steak Tartare" and ending with "Chef Joey's 'Organic Suuupriiiizzze!'" We got every-body covered here. E-V-E-R-Y-B-O-D-Y, don't ya know?"

"Hey, take care of yer bod, and yer bod'll, like, take care of you, right?" the mosquito hummed as diners began to mull their menus. "I take care of myself, let me tell ya," it might continue, to nobody in particular. Or perhaps it would declare, "I'm only here 'cause I wanna be, ya know. I don't really havta do this, right? I've got, like, this dream day job that keeps me real busy. Right? I'm a personal trainer ta the stars! An' boy do I, like, get 'em focused on their bods. But that's not all, okay? I also pass along a little lifestyle tip or two I pick up from my other contacts, right? Give my clients, like, a real zinger every now and then, yessiree Jack!"

After this warmup, the mosquito flitted elsewhere about the estab-lishment with striking quickness. Each time any of the patrons ap-peared taken by surprise to find it hovering close by, it would pick up again wherever it might have left off moments before and tables away with: "Nothin' like a good workout ta make ya feel super about yer-self. Right? Life's all about the bod, I say. Y're only as good as ya look, know what I mean-n-n-n-n? Look at me, okay? Tight thighs, no flab in these abs, lemme tell ya, an' check out this killer tush. Could I do ten hours at the gym every day or what? Up-down, up-down, in-out, in-out! Right? Like I always tell my clients, 'take care of yer bod an' yer bod'll take care of youuu!' I'm totally inta my clients, right? Sure, sometimes they get kinda stressed out over their ideal body im-age an' wonder if they'll ever, like, get there. But I just remind 'em, 'hey, no pain, no gain!' I mean ya are how ya look, 24-7-365. Or 366 in leap year, okay? Whatever. So look, 'I'm here fer allayaguys,' I tell everybody, an' I'll be there fer youuu, toooo. Right? So work up a good sweat, okay? Work up a good sweat, an' I guarantee I'll give ya the kinda self-awareness ya, like, never knew ya had! We're talkin' big-time in-touch-with-yer-bod here, right? Like, feelin' down deep whoya are and why it matters is all! All that matters in life is how ya look. Ya wanna look like a million, with a bod ta die for? Hey, youuu totally can, okay! 'Look better, feel better, be better,' I always, so, like say, 'No pain, no gain!' Right?"

At the end of an evening of such service, patrons left the restaurant in the mood for a workout right away, determined to take the mosquito's advice and get into tip-top shape before they ventured out in public again. None of them wanted to appear to others as though they didn't have a great body self-image. One that would make of their lives a ceaseless satisfaction. But more immediately, they all wanted to be in prime form the next time they found themselves at the mosquito's table.

Its "Y'er only as good as ya look, know what I mean-n-n-n-n-n?" hummed in their ears for days.

THE CORPSE

Once a naked corpse in a wildly popular "Bodies" exhibition had some things to say about the crowd milling around it.

First of all, what were these people even doing here? Each day, mobs of them pressed up against the entrance doors like shoppers on Black Friday, ready to trample one another in a rush for whatever they felt was just the thing needed to fill some gap in their lives. Fistfights were a constant threat as irritable parents accused one another of cutting into line and trying to get to the corpses on display before "my little Jimmy and Janey break into tears! They've been up all night with excitement!" As if death were the latest, must-have VR game.

And look at how these people dressed! If they had no sense of refinement themselves, couldn't they at least acknowledge that the corpses they were gawking at might have possessed some of it when alive? Did they imagine the fellow in the pose of a champion runner over there, all his muscles bared and preserved—all the beauty of a powerful body at its peak forever—did they imagine he would have stooped to wearing their stained T-shirts and loud, baggy shorts in public? Or the young woman running just ahead of him in joyful awareness of her mind and body so beautifully in balance, how thankful she must be to have escaped ending up like one of these coiffured mall frumps all about her. Like lovers on a Grecian urn the young pair looked.

Even the corpses whose organs presented various stages of disease or decay must wince at the spectacle of this squinting, grimacing throng who'd bought tickets for an opportunity to feel pleased about their own physical state by comparison. A sweaty crush barely able to resist the urge to reach out and poke at bodies so coolly poised—little did they know who, the corpses or their lot, looked the more ravaged by time, excess, and neglect.

But what struck the corpse as even more distasteful was the unacknowledged fascination with death itself betrayed by so many of these people. How clear death's power over them was as they tried to mask their fixation through graceless displays of revulsion or self-conscious titters. Rather than giving themselves over to awe at the human form fully revealed, they sought to cover up their embarrassment at its naked truth by adopting a Peeping Tom sneer, as if to satisfy a repressed necrophilic urge while still pretending they didn't suffer from it in the slightest.

This secret infatuation with death must leave them only half-alive, the corpse supposed: strangers to their own existence unless it brought them some thrill that raised their pulse a beat or two. The equivalent of Eros and Thanatos sitting side by side in life's cheap seats yet oblivious to each other's presence all the while? No wonder benumbed internet porn was the biggest business on the planet. What else could offer these people the combination of titillation and deniability that no doubt brought them to an exhibition like this as well? How prurient! And how morbid! It was enough to give any self-respecting corpse the heebie-jeebies.

This one was so offended that it wanted to shout out loud, "Who are the real dead people here, anyway?"

THE PIT BULL

Once a pit bull refused to go for the throat of every other dog around.

How had things descended to this appalling state, it shuddered with disgust? It certainly didn't bear other canines any particular malice. In a better world, the pit bull was convinced, it might even have found life-long friends among them.

But not in the world of Reality TV survival shows. That was made clear to the pit bull soon after it balked at filming one more episode of the hugely popular "Raging Mutts." It felt it needed time to reflect on whether this was really the life it wanted to lead going forward.

"Of course it is!" was the response from the whiz kid with spiky hair and a toothy smile who'd been sent out from network headquarters to troubleshoot the dog's refusal to go on with the show. "You can't quit! Not with your star power! This is the perfect vehicle for you! You're on top of the heap, so why quit now?"

"I simply don't see the value in any of this."

"Who's talking value? It's just a performance, remember."

The pit bull wasn't particularly reassured by this reply.

"Look at it this way," the whiz kid went on while picking at a pimple, "we're not dealing with an audience of Einsteins out there. We give our target demographic what market research tells us they want. And market research tells us the target demographic is getting bored of contestants acting out sham betrayals or chewing the bark off trees in front of a camera. That also goes for watching disappointed contestants attempt suicide. Audiences want something more this season."

"Like eating one's own kind on cue?"

"Believe me, none of us in Froth-at-the-Mouth Programming are comfortable with that. You think every last one of us doesn't wish we could offer more quality stuff? I got a hundred knockout ideas right here in my own head. How about this, just as one example: an "Unwanted-Baby Giveaway" contest? Problem is, viewers just don't have the attention span any longer for that level of complexity. So we have to settle for dogs eating dogs. Especially during sweeps week."

"But it's all so degrading."

34

"Of course it is! That's the beauty of it, don't you see? Giving contestants a once-in-a-lifetime chance to be a winner and then humiliating them in prime time is epic in a way. Epic!"

"But what does that do for me? I can't go on anymore making this vicious spectacle of myself. And for what? What do I get out of it?"

"Okay, okay. How about this: a six-figure book deal with the famous publishing house our parent company just bought? Corporate is already tossing about a few blockbuster titles. My favorite is 'Down and Dirty with a Real Dog.' Like it?"

"I honestly need some time to think about where all this is headed."

"Sure thing! Sure thing! Take all day if you want. You can never give these decisions too much thought. I'm with you on that, one million percent!"

THE VAMPIRE BATS

Once vampire bats came out of their caves by the millions to discharge their civic duty.

It wouldn't do to remain in their dark haunts when society's call for the execution of justice rang out. They'd been at this for a long time, after all, predating thumbs-up-thumbs-down-day at the Coliseum, stonings in the village square, serial beheadings, and the burning of witches.

With that history, they'd all but claimed the voice of public conscience in matters of guilt and innocence. Innocence mostly, for it was a sense of communal innocence that inspired any self-respecting bat to exert itself in the name of justice.

During periods when communal innocence seemed in short supply and only a few public leaders could still be counted on to claim the voice of the highest authority in dismissing pleas by the accused for mercy, vampire bats were in great demand to fill the gap and convince an unsettled populace that the old standards for inflicting punishment still held.

In this capacity, they acted for all those who couldn't make it down to the local courthouse or prison parking lot themselves to shout for vengeance upon some stranger they'd been told on some blog deserved it. More than anything else, the spectacle of swarming, screeching vampire bats served to assure the populace at large that justice by proxy was still possible, no matter how hard it might be at times to do the right thing in one's own life.

One's own life might be just too complicated for a simple decision on good and evil, but the life of a publicly identified rotter was easy to pass judgment on. And if guilt could be pinpointed in this way, then ipso facto, innocence must be just as obvious. Already there by default in everybody not currently under sentence. So bearing witness to the punishment meted out to those declared guilty was bearing witness as well to one's own personal virtue.

No wonder these gatherings at the courthouse or in the prison parking lot took on an air of ritual self-purification, after which participants could resume their everyday lives purged of emotion in a mass catharsis that renewed community bonds. In place of Aristotle's catharsis through pity and fear, one need only substitute mass rage and a conviction of one's own righteousness to experience the effect desired.

How fortunate, then, to have vampire bats show the way.

THE SCAPEGOAT

Once scapegoats were on the verge of being hunted to extinction.

Everybody wanted the head of a scapegoat to mount on their wall, it seemed. The demand had become so great that even dusty skulls and moth-eaten tatters of old hide dragged out of the nation's attics and basements were fetching unheard-of prices online. But while dead scapegoats were common enough, live specimens were rarely seen anymore as they were being driven ever and ever farther into wilderness areas.

Up here among the glacial moraines and barren crags, here where the chill air sharpened every sense and put it on alert, a lone scapegoat stood at the edge of a precipice and surveyed the valley below for tiny hunters pushing themselves beyond their natural limits to find and bag their very own scapegoat.

Why this mania? A single scapegoat trophy nailed up on view was never enough. Even a whole row might not suffice, given the current climate of rumors and envy. While to have no scapegoats at all to point to was nearly guaranteed to bring on the severest of anxieties and depressions.

Internet trolls appeared to be particularly prone to pursuing scapegoats for whatever reason and from whatever distance. In basement obscurity, they scanned their screens for targets, whether real or imagined, and then, joining cyber mobs so as to cloak themselves in perpetual anonymity, set upon their luckless victims in virtual reality. Then there were numberless others on private hunts for any scapegoat they could find to blame for their own failures, ethical debacles, serial illegalities, total incompetence, out-and-out lies, you name it.

Civic scapegoating was also on the rise. Those under local scrutiny for some act of malfeasance in office or other impropriety sought to shift the blame to "one of my staffers." While on a national level, shady politicians up for re-election might do the same (except on a broader scale) by stirring their howling base to blame any problem they themselves had created on those calling them out for doing so. And on the transnational level, scapegoat conspiracies within conspiracies within conspiracies provided the broadest cover of all for any who needed it.

Presumably, given all of these facts, the number of scapegoats left in the wild must be declining rapidly. Would a day soon come when all efforts to find one were focused on a lone survivor?

If so, when that final scapegoat had been tracked to some place like this remote precipice, would it be torn apart by competing pursuers in a brawl over who had best claim to the prize? Would gruesome hunks of their kill be triumphantly carried home in all directions? And what then? Such urgency had been placed on bagging scapegoats that their eventual demise must have dire repercussions. When no more were to be found, what would desperate scapegoat hunters do?

Take aim at each other in their uncontrollable need?

THE FOX

Once a fox came up with a foolproof entrepreneurial scheme.

Rather than follow the usual practice of selling people something they probably didn't need, the fox chose to take advantage of the marketing strategy of buying something from them that they no longer appeared to have much use for. It offered to purchase their unwanted shame. In bulk.

The fox made the following pitch to all who would listen: "Ever wanted it all, but never had the nerve to go for it? Put those days behind you. I guarantee whatever you desire in fame, fortune, sex, power, or anything else you crave in return for your shame. If shame is all that holds you back from fighting your way over others to the top and doing whatever it takes to stay there once you've made it, then hesitate no longer. Your lucky day has come! If you're not completely satisfied with this chance of a lifetime to be shame-free once and for all, I promise to return your shame in full, no questions asked. But wait, there's more! I'll even let you name your own price! Hurry, this offer ends soon."

That closing pitch was the masterstroke of the fox's strategy. It had grasped the simple truth that once the offer ended, fears of a falling price would cause even the most hesitant seller to panic into unloading any and all remaining shame for whatever it might still fetch. Nobody wanted to be stuck with shame that was worthless.

There was another phase to the fox's plan that came to be considered equally shrewd. Once it had cornered the market in what came to be known as "junk shame," the fox created a startup called "Fruits of Shame," gambling that junk shares in others' shame might still prove attractive to amateur speculators. The name had a golden allure to it, and the startup's initial public offering took off immediately, with prices reaching new highs in every trading session thereafter. On TV screens, computers, and news racks everywhere, the face of "The Market Fox" became easily the most recognizable in the land.

Despite this stunning success, the fox was troubled by an unanticipated and deepening sense of dissatisfaction. It was proving far too easy to convince people to divest themselves of shame for next to nothing. They practically begged the fox to take it, all but throwing whatever shame they might still have at its feet. There simply wasn't any challenge left in the enterprise.

Alone in newly expanded offices after a year-end celebration over beating analysts' expectations time and again (and increasingly by triple digits as individuals and corporations vied to cash out their own shame ahead of competitors), the fox brushed bits of confetti from its head and shoulders, then turned and walked away from the bright numbers scrolling across the giant stock ticker above.

"It just shouldn't be this easy," it grumbled with a disappointed expression on its face, almost as if it had tasted something sour.

IV

NARCISSUS

Once Narcissus decided to step back from the glassy water.

The pond he'd spent so much time admiring himself in had simply grown too popular of late. If you could barely see your reflection anymore (what with the pushy crowds peering at their own reflections over your shoulders), why stay?

Where did this collection of chattering newcomers intent on calling attention to themselves come from? What absolute frights most were. Was this what passed for "appeal" today, these gauche attempts to hide some nagging inner flaw, perhaps, by making a distracting spectacle of oneself? Or did they think the way to match his classic beauty was to put their ill-favored psyches on full display? For imitation to be the sincerest form of flattery, it at least had to be worthy of serious notice.

Take these clumsy teens hooting and clowning about, plus pop idols fresh from rehab (or on their way back to it), peroxide blondes tarting up their two-year-olds for the latest "Lil' Miss Pedo-Bait Pageant," soused male CEOs with their shirts open to the navel for an office party, tweet-kings striking "Il Duce" poses or grabbing the private parts of anyone within reach (to keep from falling, they typically claimed)—these and so many more cloddish slaves to self-flattery were here.

Revolted by it all, Narcissus made his decision to step back from the water. Or rather tried to step back. For as much as he strained, the counterpress of his uninvited companions proved much stronger. As did the annoyance with which they voiced their displeasure at being distracted from gazing at their own reflections by his efforts. "Who the hell do you think you are?" was how most expressed that displeasure. Or simply, "Hey, down in front, jerk!"

Barely able to maintain his balance anymore against the pressure at his back, Narcissus feared he might tumble headlong into his own image and drown. Worse, would anybody even notice if he did? Would it be as if he'd never been here at all, rooted to this spot in admiration of his unparalleled beauty? One last look at himself might be all there was time for now. One last chance to kiss his reflected lips and promise to return when he could be alone with his beauty once more. But when he searched desperately for his face, it was nowhere to be seen. Nowhere!

Just row upon row of hollow-eyed mugs grinning back at themselves.

THE DOPPELGÄNGER

Once a doppelgänger wondered what life would be like if only . . .

Catching sight of the figure everyone took to be the doppelgänger's twin always brought a jolt because of how little similarity the two seemed to have. There was, the doppelgänger had to admit, a surface resemblance, but that must happen all the time, given the boom in makeover treatments of late to turn you into the spitting image of anyone you envied.

You didn't even have to resemble others physically. Dressing or talking like them was apparently enough to show that you were kindred spirits, along with thousands of others dressing and sounding the same. While "thinking as one" with somebody else could simply be the kind of frantic "friending" that now provided an illusory defense against the terror of finding yourself alone.

The doppelgänger, by contrast, actually did want to be alone. Or at least not be confused with anybody else. There must have been something in the doppelgänger's youthful aspirations that presaged a future quite apart from this bothersome rival who had for years robbed the doppelgänger of a self that was free of outside definition.

What could be more discouraging than to be a doppelgänger in your own life? To wonder if a struggle to "know thyself" had been anything more than an illusion: a phantom quest. And whether times and places and experiences had in fact made a difference, had meant something and not been mere fantasies adopted from others to fill a void between birth and now. What other proof did the doppelgänger have of not being a mere figment of the imagination?

Thoughts such as these most often arose in the hours before dawn, when the doppelgänger sat at a window and stared through a motionless reflection at the shadowy world beyond the pane.

Soon the reflection must fade in the gathering daylight and the doppelgänger lose even this evidence of being oneself and no other. But until then, the image would still have a solidness and definition to it that were reassuring for the testimony they offered that the doppelgänger's years, even those seemingly the most unstructured, did add up to something more than just a might-have-been, a puzzle of a thousand pieces with some missing. Everything the doppelgänger had ever valued must remain in this likeness on the glass that memory helped trace. Everything still had significance. Still belonged.

As even moments like this one must, when the doppelgänger sat at the window and wondered what life would be like if only . . .

THE CUCKOOS

Once a pair of cuckoos devoted a great deal of thought to their parenting skills.

"How can we guarantee the brightest future for our precious eggs?" they asked themselves again and again. Traditionally, cuckoos have sought to advance the prospects of their young by laying them in the nests of other birds. In this way, the hatchlings might gain from varied environments and grow up to be more well-rounded and more successful than their parents.

But this pair of cuckoos differed in one important way from that pattern of behavior. Already convinced they were the most well-rounded and most successful birds they knew, they wanted their young to have every opportunity to prove they were worthy of the genes they inherited by duplicating for all the world to see what their parents had already attained.

To this end, the cuckoos diligently planned out every moment of their unhatched eggs' future: what brain-stimulating bauble to buy first, how to "ace" the entrance interviews of the most prestigious Pre-Ks for gifted toddlers, which youth soccer league to join, which higher education prep courses to enroll in, what community service looked best on college and university applications, the choicest careers for wealth and prestige, which political party to support, and so on.

Despite all these efforts, the cuckoos couldn't free themselves of a nagging anxiety that their young might not grow up to be a credit to them. Suppose the little ones turned out not to show any benefit from all these efforts to secure a future as impressive as their parents' past? Wouldn't that failure inevitably mean years of underachievement, hopelessness, and low self-esteem?

As the cuckoos looked around themselves, this anxiety about being embarrassed by their offspring was only increased by what they saw. The neighbors' clutch of eggs appeared so promising. Could their own ever hope to match the neighbors' in Pre-K-for-gifted-toddlers interviews, soccer wins, prep courses, college or university admissions, career choices, wealth and prestige, political affiliation, and so on? They even began to wonder if the neighboring eggs weren't in fact meant to be theirs all along and had inexplicably ended up in the wrong nest.

Once they'd reached this distressed state of mind, it wasn't long before the cuckoos were driven to take desperate measures. They began roaming far and wide in search of unguarded eggs that could prove worthy of their attention and love.

The many they plucked from other nests not only burdened theirs, however, but also made their own eggs appear even more unsatisfactory by comparison. In the cuckoos' eyes, the new ones definitely seemed more likely to do them honor by making something of themselves what would be fully reflective of all the parenting efforts and sacrifices made on their behalf.

This being the case, the cuckoo couple felt they had no choice posterity-wise but to begin pushing their own eggs out of the overcrowded nest, letting them fall to their fates below.

THE HOMING PIGEON

Once an elderly homing pigeon began to lose its sense of direction.

It could still manage to find the way back to its roost, but the return trip, which had always felt shorter than the journey out, now seemed the reverse, and the accustomed landmarks on which the pigeon relied had become harder to find with advancing years. Increasingly, it wandered off course, sometimes by miles, and only succeeded in righting its way through hopeful guesses at where to turn next.

When others began to remark on the homing pigeon's difficulty, it tried to laugh the matter off. So long as it fluttered back into view eventually, was there any reason for alarm? Lapses were bound to happen now and then. After decades on the wing, should there be any wonder that the many passages it had made might become crossed in its mind and lead back to places it hadn't expected?

This explanation failed to account, however, for the most puzzling aspect of the drift in the pigeon's bearings: the fact that it had no trouble at all remembering its early flights, some of which could be mentally retraced in astonishing detail. It also recalled the exact smell of inland plains many harvests ago and the feel of the wind lifting it over the first wide stretch of water it had ever crossed. Yet for all the certainty with which the pigeon could navigate its distant past, more recent years took on the drift of clouds, while last week was already dissolving into mist and what had just happened might as well have happened to strangers. Experience had ceased to cast its guiding shadow over the ground.

Even repeating again and again to itself the recollections of a lifetime in hopes of keeping them as clear as the day they'd been fixed in the pigeon's mind proved misleading. Instead of reassurance, the attempt often brought gasps of pained surprise at what had once been taken for certain, then lost to memory, then encountered again only by chance. And what was not recovered in this haphazard way vanished from the pigeon's life story altogether, as though the missing pages had been declared a forgery and not worthy of note.

Could memory become such a pitiless foe—this lifelong friend that turned out to betray one (a stranger now, waiting for the moment of one's greatest need of reassurance and then coldly pretending not to have heard the heart's plea at all)?

Nor were the pigeon's loving mate and young, circling in patterns they hoped might point the way home, able to slow the steady wasting away of a soul that had guided their own affections for so long. Leaving them helpless before dazed questions of "Who are you?" and "Why are you here?"

What reassurance could they offer the struggling homing pigeon that would ever bring it back across the fading terrain once familiar to them all?

SPIRIT AND FLESH

Once Spirit and Flesh were directed to undergo relationship counseling.

Years of mutual suspicion and often bitter conflict—when they weren't determined simply to ignore one another—had alienated the pair to the point where the only thing they could agreed upon was that this feuding couldn't continue much longer without destroying them both. Flesh charged Spirit with constantly putting on condescending airs or else drifting off into hazy musings intended to shield it from even acknowledging the existence of Flesh. While in Spirit's view, Flesh was intent on embarrassing it at every turn by indulging in mindless pleasures, from the inane to the utterly debased.

Relations between the two had reached such a point, in fact, that even being in each other's company was an ordeal. And their only relief on those occasions when either party hinted at "ending it all" increasingly lay in sleeping pills for the one and going on a week-long sensual binge for the other, anything that would deaden the pain suffered by both.

Given this history, relationship counseling was, in itself, risky business. So much could go so wrong so quickly, beginning with the demand each made that the other be thoroughly searched for concealed weapons when entering the first counseling session. To such a point had trust between Spirit and Flesh fallen.

Things could have been different. The two didn't have to travel down this road. There'd been plenty of chances to get things right. Spirit could have shown a little more understanding, and Flesh could have insisted a little less on its own desires. But like a scab that itches and itches until scratching makes it a scar, their differences hardened over time into grudges for which there seemed no remedies.

Now they found themselves on opposite sides of a recently polished table and stared down at their own reflections for a full five minutes so as to avoid looking at each other. While the appointed relationship counselor prepared to do for them what they'd proven unable to accomplish on their own.

There sat Spirit, debating internally how to project confidence about the outcome of the process without appearing aloof and insensitive. This effort would turn out to be more difficult than Spirit had anticipated, and not simply because of the indignity of being in a situation it found demeaning. Matters wouldn't have come to such a point if the superiority of Spirit over Flesh that so many publicly proclaimed was honored by them in private to the same degree. But no, once the lights were turned out, high-mindedness went dark just as quickly, everywhere.

More troubling to Spirit at the moment, though, were the waves of queasiness brought on by a deep but unacknowledged claustrophobia that made it impossible to turn from the gathering threat mirrored in the shiny tabletop as the walls and ceiling seemed to ooze closer. It took all of Spirit's increasingly taxed powers of self-control to summon a show of sang-froid and keep from crying out, "I must have room to breathe! Freedom to soar!"

Across the table slouched Flesh, troubled by a growing anxiety about what this compulsory counseling might portend for the two of them. Flesh was fully aware that the public typically lauded Spirit with glowing terms like "noble" or "sublime" while deriding Flesh's own gifts as "base," "blind," "weak," or even "demonic." Yet how thin that regard for Spirit actually was, more honored in flowery praise than in true allegiance. Called to follow Spirit and abandon all their worldly desires for higher rewards, many people demanded to know in advance the "exact value" of what they'd gain by doing so.

In addition, the preoccupations of Flesh were more or less of a whole by contrast with those of Spirit, whose attention often appeared to be scattered all over the place. Flesh might well have yielded to the temptation to exploit its greater "unity of self" relative to Spirit's frequent turmoil, were it not for the worry that any move to gain from this advantage came at the risk of upsetting the delicate balance they'd at least managed to maintain through their difficult patches until now.

The fact was, they needed each other. How would people recognize Spirit without Flesh, since they'd grown accustomed to thinking of the two in opposition? And for Flesh, mightn't separation from Spirit turn out to be just as dicey in terms of maintaining Flesh's own sense of self? They had become an "item" in the eyes of the public, whether they liked it or not. Who would take seriously the existence of either one if asked to accept the other's reality on mere say-so? Being recognized as the real thing was hard enough already, what with all

51

the spiritual poseurs and serial exhibitionists out there clamoring for attention and getting it.

Spirit and Flesh had long since settled for a testy bond of convenience, there was no denying. And neither of them felt seriously hampered by the resulting open relationship, despite their recurrent discord. Furthermore, whatever others might think about them individually or as a twosome wasn't necessarily the truth, nor of much importance, really. More often than not, what the public saw as "Spirit" and "Flesh" was what it wanted to see, so each of them was at liberty to pursue new yearnings and new attachments with a view to a more satisfying life for itself and more latitude for the other. It might appear as though Flesh gained most from this arrangement at times and at times Spirit did. Yet time itself was a great equalizer and didn't play favorites in the long run. Why not leave it to time, then, to sort things out? What need did they really have for this unwelcome mediation session, the pair silently asked themselves simultaneously?

Just at this moment, the relationship counselor startled both Spirit and Flesh with a loud "Ahem," followed by: "As I see it, resolving this little problem the two of you seem to be having shouldn't be difficult at all."

THE OLD GOAT

Once an old goat nearly overdosed on ED pills.

That it even felt the need of such pills baffled many who knew the old goat. It certainly didn't have a history of difficulties that might have suggested such a remedy was called for. Quite the opposite, its reputation for energetic and unflagging performance was well known, legendary in fact. Ironically, the old goat's reputation may have been the very source of its troubles.

It hadn't given much thought to the matter in the past. "Either you've got what it takes or you don't" might have summed up the amount of concern the old goat had shown for what was so much a part of its nature as scarcely to deserve mention.

But that was before it started hearing stories around the office water cooler about "steamy nooners" involving many staff members, apparently. Then a mid-level colleague abandoned a marriage of twenty-five years to "find my youth again" in the back seat of roving taxis. What was going on? Maybe it was time to take the question of its reputation more seriously.

There was something demeaning, though, about having to prove your status as "numero uno" when there should have been no question about it. The goat didn't really know where to begin or how to proceed, so little thought had it given the matter in the past. But now, increasingly, its attention wandered during meetings with important clients to a muddle of shopping plans for gaudy shirts, gold-plated neck chains, and spice-scented breath sprays, along with various strategies for brushing up against curvaceous new hires in the elevator as though by accident.

When it caught itself one day trying to read the small print on packages of hair restorer and whisker dye, the old goat realized how far and how fast it was spiraling out of control. This couldn't go on. Deciding a bold step was in order, the goat made an appointment with a doctor.

"I see cases like yours all the time," the doctor said with a reassuring tone.

"You do, doc?" the goat asked in alarm. Had it actually underestimated the number of younger goats preparing to push it aside, then?

"Yes, although there wasn't much to be done about the condition until recently. Fortunately, it now has a medical designation: OGS, or Old Goat Syndrome. And when there's a name for a condition, there's a pill. Thank the pharmaceutical industry for that. Simply take one of these sample pills and call me in the morning if you experience a sudden loss in vision or hearing, as these may be signs of a side effect called RYEOAYEO, otherwise known as 'rutting your eyes out and your ears off.' To avoid long-term injury, seek immediate medical assistance for an erection lasting more than four hours."

"Are you out of your mind, doc? Medical assistance is about the last thing I'll be seeking for a four-hour erection, believe me!"

The goat did have one last question, though: "I guess I should ask you, doc, are these pills right for me?"

"They're right for everybody. Emerging research suggests Old Goat Syndrome doesn't discriminate when it strikes. Political leaders, sports and entertainment idols, movers and shakers of commerce, right down to the guy next door, you name it. Soon much of the country may be relying on these pills."

This information did nothing to calm the old goat's anxiety. The entirety of its self-image was now at stake, it feared. With these pills, half the planet could soon be laying claim to the old goat's long-standing reputation, strutting about like Priapus Unchained. To retain its position at the top, then, would it have to make an extra effort? Better leave nothing to chance in that case. Scarcely out of the doctor's office, the old goat gulped down the entire bottle of pills.

When the doctor's telephone rang the next morning, it wasn't the old goat calling but rather the police. They had a few questions they needed to ask about a suspect they were holding in a string of indecent exposure complaints at locations ranging from daycare centers to assisted living facilities.

THE MIGRATORY BIRD

Once a migratory bird stopped by the local travel agency.

The year was getting on into fall, and the bird's thoughts had begun to turn to warmer places again. This time, however, the familiar destinations just didn't seem to have the attraction they once had. The bird was tired of group tours and even of glossy fliers from its alma mater's alumni association, which had apparently downplayed scholarship fundraising to concentrate instead on providing wealthy graduates a choice of "unforgettable Wanderlust experiences" in 7-day, 14-day, and 21-day packages.

So when it noticed a poster of a deserted tropical beach taped to the window of the travel agency, the bird went straight on in and up to one of the agents appearing to be from somewhere like the place in the poster. Nothing beats first-hand knowledge, the bird told itself.

No sooner had it mentioned the poster, though, than the agent replied nonchalantly, "That place was booked up months ago."

"Months ago?" the bird asked in crestfallen surprise.

"Yes. Everybody wants to get away to a remote beach in the tropics these days."

"But the beach is empty."

"Isn't Photoshop amazing? You'd never know the place was actually packed with sunbathers, would you, or that just steps away from the beach, booked-up tourist hotels were squeezed together?"

"Well, what else have you got?" the disappointed bird asked.

"What are you looking for, exactly?"

"How can I put it? A change in my life's focus, an adventure for the senses, a rebirth of the soul, a whole new approach to the mysteries of being, a—"

"What does all that have to do with tropical beaches?" the agent broke in with a tone of having heard it all before.

"You are aware of Paul Gauguin, I assume," was the bird's miffed response.

"Are you expecting to see his ghost sitting in a Club Med beach chair?"

"Of course not, but ahhh Tahiti! Tahiti! Doesn't the word simply ring with the call of the exotic? Like Mandalay! Or Samarkand! Or

Shangri-La!"

"The kind of Shangri-La you're looking for doesn't exist, I'm afraid."

"I know that! But someplace like it where everything is inscrutable and ageless and I can get in touch with elemental truths that are denied me here."

"And what might those 'elemental truths' be?"

"That's where I need your help, don't you see? I feel I've got to open myself to raw experience while I still can and have hot blood drum through my veins in the dusky night. Go native and get in a little all-night flocking with birds of a different feather, if you get my drift. . . You do get my drift, don't you?"

"We don't run sex tours."

"Oh, don't get me wrong! Don't get me wrong! I'm talking about something magical! A mystical transformation of the self! Getting in touch with ancient teachings and the inner me! Becoming one with universal rhythms! Embracing the 'Eternal Feminine'! Why, everything you must feel in your very bones! You're from those sultry climes, aren't you?"

"What makes you think that? I was born here."

"Here? You're not from there? Come now, you're just kidding, aren't you? I see in your face everything to make me come alive, truly alive, everything that is waiting out there somewhere for me, beckoning . . . always beckoning . . . like that poster in the window!"

"That poster isn't the real thing, I tell you."

"It has to be the real thing! Don't you understand, I have needs here! Needs only paradise can satisfy!"

THE BUTTERFLY AND THE MOTH

Once a butterfly fell in love with a moth.

Why that happened defied explanation. The butterfly was like the coming of spring. April played in its wings, and their soft flutter made the air glow. When it would light a moment on a blade of grass or a twig, that place, however small, rivaled rainbows.

The moth had none of this magic. It faltered through life as though its wings were an accident. And this accident the moth took as a cruel affront. It was a low trick of nature that it found itself with ungainly wings, quite apart from the added insult of its drab, puffy bulk.

Nor was the moth merely awkward physically. It got in its own way all the time emotionally as well. What other being had to endure the mortifications it did every day, the moth groaned? Life was nothing more than a long bad joke, and the moth was the constant butt of it. The whole of its experience seemed designed solely to deny the moth any dignity it might aim for.

The butterfly recognized the moth's pained discontent but loved it all the more for that. Perhaps the moth's bitterness at having been slighted by life was the very thing that proved irresistible.

Even when the moth's frustrations caused it to turn on the butterfly, as if blaming it for a magnificence that put the moth itself in a worse light by comparison, the butterfly's love never wavered. At such times, it would fold close its splendor to avoid upsetting the moth any further or else quiet the lilting grace of its flight.

It wasn't that the moth meant to hurt the butterfly. And it wasn't that the butterfly didn't feel hurt, sometimes terribly hurt. The moth saw the pain it caused but couldn't help itself. While the butterfly saw how cruelly love was repaid but also couldn't help itself.

Day after day, the moth blundered about and cursed its lot, while the butterfly followed lovingly behind, refusing to use its own luminous wings to fly away. It was truly a mystery.

*

In another version of this story, it was the moth that fell in love with the butterfly and tried in every way to be near the object of its

57

affections. This devotion was a torment, the moth often acknowledged to itself sadly, for in the presence of the butterfly, it was convinced it must appear a hundred times more ugly than if it simply kept to itself and abandoned love completely.

All of the misgivings it had, the dull heaviness it felt in its heart whenever it tried to imagine a lifetime spent with the butterfly, might have been expected to dissuade the moth from its suit. How could it ever be worthy of sharing even a moment with this extraordinary being? Wasn't that desire just a hopeless delusion that could only lead to disaster? The moth half feared that if it ever realized its dreams and won the butterfly's love, it might not survive the bliss.

The butterfly, for its part, was barely aware of the moth's existence. The earnest suitor's attempts to call attention to itself while at the same time trying desperately to hide its shortcomings appeared to the butterfly as merely a puzzling blur in the air, a bothersome distraction. That the blur might be the sole expression an awkward constancy could manage never crossed the butterfly's mind. While helpless before the burning marvel of its love, the moth circled ever closer and closer.

This second version of the story was a mystery too.

THE WOOD DUCKS

Once a pair of wood ducks grew old together.

It had been a long life they'd shared, a life not without its challenges. In truth, love—owing so much to chance already—might never have brought the two birds together in the first place. Being born on different continents in the wide scattering of wood duck populations made the likelihood of their ever meeting remote beyond calculation. What circumstances must ultimately have brought them together could only be guessed at by other ducks on the lake.

Without question, they made for a strange couple in the eyes of many. These two didn't just mate for life as wood ducks customarily do but often appeared so focused on each other as to be unaware that other ducks were even around. They might come out of their love-trance every once in a while and fall in with the flock as it traced familiar patterns across the lake, only to veer off again into their private rushes and reeds or take wing to a secret love nest in some hollow tree.

What were they up to after vanishing like that, others in the flock wondered? It must involve more than the conjugal routines that the rest of them took as the normal course of a couple's life. The array of avian erotic moves they imagined with a wink and a nod would only have made the absent pair smile at such limits to imagination.

Admittedly, the two had felt an irresistible attraction at first sight, yet this by itself couldn't explain their abiding attachment ever since. Hatching out on opposite sides of the globe had colored their lives differently and might well have hindered a shared life going forward, but the contrary became the embracing reality of all their years together.

Their pasts had steadily merged, until they found themselves at one, paddling side by side or flying wing to wing for days on end through borderlands between their origins that were thought uncrossable by other ducks. In that expanse without boundaries, whatever self-awareness one had, the other shared. Whatever one experienced, the other experienced just as fully. And when they soared together from the lake and headed for the borderlands, the pleasure they took in the realm they were entering was simultaneous, equal, complete.

V

DOTS

Once dots complained about all the attempts made to connect them.

The result, they declared, invariably turned out to be a maladroit, unconvincing scratchwork that required a caption in order to be recognized for what it supposedly represented. "Oh, so that's it," was the most common response to being told how connecting the dots revealed a pattern in them, followed by a confused "And here I was convinced the whole thing was nothing more than a child's doodling."

Not that those taking credit for the latest connection of dots were daunted by this mistaking of the grand designs they'd traced out for a mere child's doodling yet again. Some degree of confusion was actually of benefit to regular dot-connectors, for it meant they remained indispensable to any discussion of how to discover grand designs in what might otherwise be judged an aimless mess. At least until people grew impatient with the whole thing and turned to a fresh scattering of dots to puzzle over. And once again, those who considered themselves experts at interpreting dots and doodles might be counted on to offer their services.

No wonder dots got fed up. For dots, despite what might be inferred from their seeming uniformity, prided themselves on being distinct and independent. They had no difficulty telling one another apart, so why shouldn't they take offense at being lumped together under some catchall assumption about what they shared? Left to themselves, they might avoid each other's company altogether and quite happily shun the conformity imposed by connection to others in favor of the liberty to follow their own designs wherever these might lead them—even if this liberty offered no pattern to assign a recognizable meaning—nothing, ultimately, to separate "grand design" from "aimless mess."

Maybe dots didn't have a collective meaning and didn't need one.

Maybe they were just dots. Wasn't that enough? Did the lack of a shared meaning prove that no meaning existed? Or might it merely suggest the limited vision of the meaning-seekers?

Even the smallest dot held coiled within it the promise of this, that, everything, or even nothing. And then to have some self-declared know-it-all who'd long since dismissed this magical ambiguity in favor of the reassurance of "the known"—for the comfort of certainty when certainty came at the cost of all else—to have that know-it-all, out of a personal yet unacknowledged inadequacy perhaps, seek to impose an understanding on whatever still retained the glory of the undefined— never! A mere smudge of a dot would rebel at such a travesty.

Not that rebelling did much good. For "meaning," once the slightest pattern has been spied in anything, is merciless and can crush the life out of whatever it fastens upon.

In the end, the dots never stood a chance.

THE MANTIS

Once a mantis gained quite a reputation for "storytelling journalism," specifically through grieving-victim interviews.

Both quick and confident, the mantis benefited from a highly developed instinct for detecting any vulnerability in those it interviewed and for turning that weakness into a compelling "narrative" it could then pass on to its audience. Once targeted by the mantis, any recipient of its attention might expect the inevitable.

"I understand how painful and tragic this must be for you, and I certainly don't wish to be intrusive or to make things worse," the mantis would typically begin in emotive tones and with a mesmerizing gaze, "but could you share with our audience, up close and personal, just how painfully tragic life is for you right now?"

"I really don't feel like talking about it."

"Of course you don't. I understand and fully respect that, and I certainly would not want to increase your suffering in the slightest way, so just between you and me, how would you describe that suffering, in detail? Take your time if need be."

"What good would describing my suffering in detail do?"

"It might not seem like a lot at the moment, but in the long run, it could help our audience draw an inspirational lesson from your heartrending ordeal and feel that warm sense of uplift that has become so essential to the public these days."

"Have you yourself ever grieved in public? Torn your heart open for all to see? What does my personal anguish have to do with their need to feel uplifted?"

"Certainly not as much as it has to do with you and the private agony you're going through right now, don't misunderstand me, but helping us see what a wrenching experience like the one you've been through has meant personally should help others process their own future traumas more quickly."

"How?"

"By providing an unforgettable illustration of something very, very important these days. Wouldn't it help you put your own grief in perspective and feel better personally to know that others found in your devastating pain the strength to feel less devastated by whatever pain they themselves might have?"

"When?"

"Anytime. Wouldn't that be worth something?"

"What?"

"Well, worth your having had to suffer through everything in silence up till now. Hasn't that been worse than anything else, not sharing your misfortune? Here's a chance to tell your heartrending story to millions out there listening and watching. Making it real for them."

"Who?"

"The largest audience in the history of grieving-victim programming, we estimate."

"Where?"

"Everywhere you're being heard and seen at this very moment. Living rooms, neighborhood bars, big-box stores, treadmill rooms at fitness clubs, airport waiting lounges, the biggest digital screen in Times Square, all across social, you name it. After this interview, you and your heartrending ordeal are sure to become household words, true beacons of inspiration and hope. All you have to do is spend a few minutes telling the world out there about the unimaginably painful ordeal you're going through and how much it's tested your faith but then ultimately made you stronger and how much you now realize the importance of the little things we all take for granted in life and how much you've grown because of your personal tragedy and how you couldn't have made it without the support of others and how going public like this with one's private agony is such a big, big part of taking today's healing process to a whole new level for everybody and—"

"Why? And why are you doing this to me?"

THE MARCH OF THE PUNDITS

Once a film crew set out to document the march of the pundits.

The intent had been to capture this unique phenomenon for posterity by venturing deep into pundit habitat, braving the barren wasteland they traditionally favored and the mind-numbing chill of its windier reaches. All this in the darkness that covered the pundit world for months at a time.

The logistical aspects of the effort were understandably daunting. Simply getting to a place so remote, so devoid of any sign of sentient life, was fraught with difficulties. Terrain that might at first be thought solid and certain turned out more often than not simply frozen in place, prone to sudden collapse or, being deeply cracked beneath the surface, to breaking loose with an ear-splitting roar and carrying the unsuspecting away.

Everywhere in this vast emptiness lay the stiff remains of pundits who'd become disoriented, gotten hopelessly lost, and been given up for dead long since. And dead they most definitely appeared, despite the hint of an eerie flicker in their glazed eyeballs on occasion. Months passed before the filmmakers actually spotted a "live one" waddling about in the distance and showing at least minimal signs of life, though whether that be intelligent life or not remained unclear.

Cautiously tracking this curious figure along its erratic path, all the while nearly driven to distraction by its frequent reversals and long, circular meanderings over ground it had already covered time and time again, the exhausted crew finally came upon what they'd nearly given up hope of ever finding. There in the distance one teeth-chattering day, amounting to no more than a dim, undifferentiated mass at first, wheeled a great huddle of pundits bearing hard upon one another to preserve what little inner fire each still possessed then taking it in turns to suffer the gales that buffeted their outer ranks and valiantly do their part to safeguard the entire community locked in what came to be dubbed "the scrum that saves."

It was this commitment to mutual self-preservation that proved most astonishing in the documentary that ultimately grew out of the expedition. Audiences who had rarely taken much notice of pundits other than to chuckle on occasion at their rather comical demeanor (suggestive of inveterate tipplers trying to stagger home without falling down and, when that inevitably happened, pushing themselves the rest of the way on their bellies), these same audiences felt a surge of more troubling emotions when confronted with 50-foot, 3D pundits on an IMAX screen.

The spectacle was overwhelming. Not only the solid wall of puffed-up determination but also the unflappable confidence shown by each of these strange birds that regardless of any differences they might have, from snits of the moment to abiding enmity, they stood united to the last pundit on one thing: ensuring the survival of their kind despite all that reason might lead any observer to expect.

THE GARGOYLES

Once, determined to boost lackluster viewership counts, producers of a news-and-opinion program signed up two gargoyles.

The program needed to raise audience interest, the producers had concluded. Nobody stayed glued to plodding, in-depth discussions of issues crucial to the survival of the Republic anymore. To begin with, who could define "in-depth" in a way the show's followers would understand and, furthermore, who cared if you could or not?

Even earsplitting *ad hominem* attacks on opponents, long a staple of the show, now sounded "so out of date." Surveys of faithful viewers showed they were just as likely to shout at the screen with the volume off as turned up. The same was true for hammering their smartphones in "let us know what you think" responses to questions about a news-maker's politics, private life, or potential risk of indictment. Having "the right optics" and "immediate impact" held more promise of an uptick in ratings. Thus the decision to bring on the gargoyles.

When they were first rolled into the studio and positioned opposite one another, members of the production team held their collective breath. What would the audience response be? Would mere ghoulish grimacing be enough? Would viewers be satisfied with that and not demand more? Would it be the kiss of death that the gargoyles weren't saying anything, intelligible or otherwise? As the on-screen response meter lit up, though, everyone could exhale with relief and give each other high fives all around. Clearly it didn't matter in the least that the gargoyles hadn't said anything. Derision, misrepresentation, false analogies, red herrings, sniggering innuendo, outright slurs and blatant lies—none of these equaled the impact of gargoyles silently pulling faces at each other and at the audience.

The saving in production costs was obvious. But equally obvious was the realization that even the fast-talking, high-paid hosts of these programs could be replaced in a flash by rigid ideologue-grotesques, bringing even further savings. Every day and every night, simply propping up a cardboard host in place of a flesh-and-blood one would provide all the introduction needed for the gargoyles as the true stars of the show: tirelessly scowling caricatures of thought caked in bird droppings.

THE BOOBY AND THE LOON

Once a booby and a loon hosted a Talk Radio show.
End of story.

THE QUESTION MARK

Once it was proposed that the question mark be declared obsolete.

"What purpose does it serve anymore?" was the common objection to the question mark's continued use in an age that increasingly got by very well with emojis, all-caps acronyms, sentence fragments, and the exclamation point—the exclamation point above all else.

The comma, semicolon, and colon were on their way out already: curious oddities that fewer and fewer people could either explain or find a use for in the new climate of hyper-emphatic expression. Ideas that required more than a single sentence were now being crowded out by slogans seemingly intended to convince through blunt-force trauma. Even the period was in trouble. It was saved only by the fact that eventually all things must end.

But the exclamation point, now there was punctuation up to the demands of the day! With everybody who engaged in public debate bent on dominating all opponents and any exchange being only a few syllables away from an outburst of expletives, threats, or sophomoric jeers, forgoing the exclamation point was a sure sign of not being firm in one's convictions.

To some, force in punctuation was literally a measure of their expressive vigor, and among these, the flaccid question mark looked like the very symbol of impotence. There were no such concerns about the exclamation point, always standing straight and tall. It was here to stay as the only sure means of demonstrating that one was right about absolutely everything, from personal taste to social issues to religious convictions and so on. When the intent was to avoid betraying the slightest self-doubt amid a swirl of conflicting certainties, nothing else could serve the purpose half so well.

The danger of self-doubt, in the end, was the very reason so many thought the question mark should be abandoned. Any admission that you didn't already know as much as you ever needed to know, that what you were absolutely certain about yesterday might not be so clear today, that abiding enigmas might form as much of our inner workings as those of the cosmos at large—acknowledging any of these possibilities was a sign of weakness to be avoided at all costs.

Clearly, the question mark must go!!

HARM'S WAY

Once there was considerable dispute about the exact location of "Harm's Way."

This was despite the fact that the phrase "in harm's way" was on the lips of nearly everyone, from national and international leaders all the way down to a pedestrian looking both ways before jaywalking. Yet anybody seeking to inquire where exactly "Harm's Way" might be found typically received a flurry of contradictory responses.

"It's in that direction."

"No, this direction."

"Are you both blind, it's clearly right over there."

"You're all wrong. Can't you see two inches in front of your faces?"

Conflicts of opinion on this order often started small but quickly drew large crowds, with heated divisions spreading everywhere as neighbor turned from neighbor and even family members from one another in spluttering frustration. To say nothing of the age-old differences of opinion between generations, communities, nations, and ultimately entire cultures that grew increasingly pronounced as the whereabouts of "Harm's Way" became ever more obscure. Like historical disputes over the legitimacy of *"terra incognita"* and *"Here Be Monsters"* scrawled on fading maps, these larger wrangles could prove long-lasting, were it not for the eruption of a new disagreement that refocused everyone's attention on yet another claim to have discovered the true location of "Harm's Way."

Given this state of affairs, concern grew that if some form of unanimity was not reached, and soon, virtually every spot on Earth might become "Harm's Way" by default. So an international commission was hurriedly formed, complete with famous dignitaries and enormous staffs, to negotiate a document of understanding on "Harm's Way" acceptable to all. The opening ceremonies for such a momentous endeavor went well enough, for there were all the customary formalities and protocols to observe. These succeeded in keeping differences in check under the established strictures of statesmanship. However, once actual deliberations got underway, it became apparent that none of the participants were willing to pinpoint "Harm's Way" in any definite manner that might reflect badly upon their own portion of the globe. Almost daily, entire delegations got up and walked out of the negotiations in protest against other nations' views, only to return hastily when it became evident their objection had fallen on deaf ears and some crucial decision might be made in their absence that would designate their own homeland as "Harm's Way in Perpetuity." Now was not the time to stand on mere principle or to be timorous in the face of such a dire threat.

It might have been argued that a universal agreement to declare a moratorium on overuse of the expression "in harm's way" as shorthand for whatever felt alien to one's own world-view could have lowered distrust and eventually led at least to a quasi-truce based on mutual civility, good will, and some attempt to understand the situations of others.

Unfortunately, what few and feeble efforts were made in this vein led nowhere. Too much was demanded in order to do what would have been necessary, at whatever level, from highest diplomacy to a squabble in the street. While by contrast, the familiar shorthand was so very convenient. And again, at all the same levels from highest diplomacy to squabbles in the street. Until not a patch of ground anywhere hadn't been labeled "Harm's Way" once or twice at a minimum, and some many times more than that.

Ultimately, one didn't have to point in any particular direction whatsoever when making the claim, since all directions were assumed to be implied and a simple whirling of the arms would suffice.

Between the default cliché and the mechanical gestures, few of those raising constant alarms paused to consider the possibility that "Harm's Way" might not lie someplace out there beyond their comfort zone but rather deep within the darkest regions of their own minds.

THE BIG LIE

Once a Big Lie considered demanding equal time.

Just how many small lies should the world be expected to swallow, the Big Lie wondered? They seemed to be everywhere, these laughable attempts to mislead. Not that such piddling falsehoods amounted to much more than a nuisance when taken singly, but since one lie typically led to another, in time the thickening odor of mendacity could pose a genuine public danger, from isolated gagging in private to bouts of mass retching that affected entire swaths of an unsuspecting population.

You could hardly draw breath anymore without choking on some truly trifling pretense or other. To say nothing of the puffed-up umbrage directed at fact checkers who'd caught out patently inept liars: total amateurs whose only refuge when trapped in some clumsy deceit was to claim they were the victim of a devious plot to take their every word "out of context."

In short, there was a surplus of dime-a-dozen lies but few real whoppers anymore. Soon people might not even be able to tell the difference, the Big Lie feared, and if things reached such a pass, wouldn't full-blown deception be cheapened and lose its claim to serious consideration? What a state of affairs that would present.

No, the time had clearly come for a return to lies with the power to make one shudder rather than simply feel embarrassed by their carnival-barker presumption of public gullibility. Lies so great that what seemed to be half of the citizenry might go red in the face shouting rabid support for them. And here the Big Lie was ready, willing, and able to step forward and restore faith in any number of falsehoods that had lost their edge and thus no longer had the potential to fool even some of the people all of the time.

But where to begin? Therein lay precisely the uncertainty that called for the overwhelming strength only a Big Lie could muster. Any miscalculation—the slightest mismatch between the need for fabrication and the fabrication itself—could spell failure, possibly on the oft-cited "unprecedented scale."

Because the distinction between true fake and false fake could be difficult to identify with certainty, due care must be taken. The lines separating 1) internet hucksterism and lies so trivial they make even petty thieves blush from 2) voice-over TV adverts implying in soporific tones that a 30-second list of wonder-drug side effects that ends with "rarely resulting in death" is no cause for alarm from 3) the latest solemn pledges before yet another congressional committee that the stock market always has the nation's interests at heart from 4) the truly dreary spectacle of "down-home" political guys with their sleeves rolled up claiming "I'm just here to carry out the people's business" as they run through a litany of equivocations and justifications in voices ranging from snide whines to what resembles barely controlled acid reflux from 5) the type of head-of-state bombast that leads people to demonize everybody else in their nation and nations to take swings at one another like thugs in the dark—these and countless additional lines of separation, once blurred, might never again be redrawn! Were the consequences of such a dire possibility not obvious?

They were to the Big Lie as it weighed whether it should press for equal time immediately or wait until all those who'd come to rely on penny-ante shams and mere slight-of-mind dishonesty no longer found in these the answer to their needs and were ready to bow their heads and bend their knees in pledging their blind fealty to the real thing once again: the truly monstrous lie.

It had happened in the past, hadn't it, even within recent memory? So why couldn't it happen again?

FEAR

Once fear disappeared.

Just packed up and headed out one fine morning for parts unknown. Those who'd been the familiars of fear were stunned at this uncharacteristic move. After all the time they'd spent in fear's company, how could it just leave them like this, without warning or farewell? How were they to get on with their lives in its absence? What would a day without fear be?

Missing-fear reports soon appeared in print and electronic media across the nation as well as on billboards and countless neighborhood power poles, but to no avail. The longer its whereabouts went unaccounted for, the deeper the public uneasiness became. People had grown so accustomed to its presence in their lives. Fear of the known as much as the unknown. Fear of the truth and fear of lies. Fear of danger and failure and rejection, of course, but equally of success and responsibility. Fear of strangers but of one's neighbor as well. Fear of the rich and powerful and fear of the homeless. Fear of the immigrant and fear of the nativist. Fear of science's challenges to religion and of religious zealotry that denies science. Fear of the devil and fear of one's own demons. Fear, in sum, as the one constant in life as people had come to know it.

Fear had never let the nation down before. People's entire existence might suddenly have to be rethought and all the old certainties be abandoned. But new alarms and suspicions could take time to develop, to say nothing of how long it might be before they became second nature to one and all. The absence of fear wasn't just inconvenient, therefore; it was a personal and public calamity.

So when fear returned unannounced one fine day, the rejoicing was boundless. Multitudes danced in the streets. Fireworks filled the nighttime sky. No explanation for the absence of fear was offered and none was asked for. Who would be so foolish as to risk driving fear away again with awkward questions? Grand parades were organized everywhere, complete with marching bands and banners that read "Welcome Home Fear!"

Everyone breathed a sigh of relief now that life was returning to normal.

VI

PAVLOV'S DOGS

Once Pavlov's dogs nearly died of acute dehydration.

After making their famous contribution to science, they'd enjoyed what was a well-deserved but brief retirement. It ended when they were beseeched to exercise their skills in the political arena as well. With election campaigns growing longer and longer, exhausted candidates and supporters looked to the dogs to provide that certain something necessary to carry the day.

Being trucked about from one political rally or photo op to another and expected to salivate on command at whatever they heard a candidate say caused serious strain to the dogs' vaunted glands over time, however. Drooling on cue wasn't as easy as political operatives seemed to think it was.

The responsibility became so taxing and so stressful, in fact, that teams of volunteers had to be recruited in towns large and small to form water brigades and keep these valuable mouths well primed. It wouldn't do to have them suddenly dry up just at the critical pitch in a stump speech, the point at which a candidate looked out into the camera lights and uttered, clear as a bell, the slogan so extensively crowd-tested for maximum effect.

The dogs strained valiantly to respond to even the least of a candidate's remarks as if it contained the sum total of advanced thinking since the dawn of humanity. Nevertheless, as the months wore on and demand for their services grew, it became impossible to keep up with the increasingly urgent requests and then abject pleas made by various campaign chiefs of staff. A point was reached when Pavlov's dogs just didn't have any more to give. They'd slavered their all for the cause.

One especially grueling night, after hours of arid assertions by a particularly long-winded candidate, the dogs finally seemed headed for the inescapable: death by political desiccation. As they began sinking one after another to the floor, their tongues, once so smooth and slick, lolled out of their mouths like rubbery blisters. Mere skin and bones now, the dogs looked as though they might crumble away to nothing if they so much as swallowed hard.

The idea that heroic first responders would be able to fight their way through a packed arena to render assistance to the wheezing dogs was out of the question. In addition, few of the sign-waving, wildly cheering party loyalists bussed in from miles around knew what to do. They certainly hadn't bargained on the sight of their canine partners dropping dead during the best part of "the speech."

The shock of the spectacle rippled in every direction through the crowd, reaching all the way to the candidate's advisors on stage. There, the chief of staff realized at once what must be done. As if by common reflex, back through the hall rippled the chief of staff's appeal to the dumbfounded assembly, with an effect that was astonishing. On every side, heads steadily disappeared from view as row after row went down on hands and knees in a spontaneous demonstration of support for these failing troupers so crucial to the final stages of the campaign.

It was quite a sight—the vast hall united in a single heartfelt moment of determination: men, women, party operatives and big-time contributors alike, even the chief of staff and the anxious candidate, abandoning all restraint and drooling as one as if the country's future depended upon it.

THE BUFFOONS

Once two troops of lowland buffoons squared off on a patch of ground where the halls of Congress now stand.

The dispute involved one of those bitter conflicts over territory and dominance that regularly arose at that time, whether originating from within the ranks of the Greater Buffoons or the Lesser.

As usual, each troop of buffoons was persuaded it alone had hereditary right to what both claimed. And so intent were both on maintaining such claims that the ground actually at issue, though quite small and shrinking all the time, assumed ever-greater importance in all eyes.

The confrontation itself also began as such confrontations regularly did, with a series of ritual feints and gestures that became more pronounced as both troops grew bolder in asserting their primacy.

While telling the two sides apart could be difficult enough under ordinary circumstances, the sight of each other brought out behavior that made it even more so. And because each troop had a limited repertoire of instinctive moves very much like the other troop's, differentiating between these buffoons came down primarily to variations in the color of certain portions of their anatomy, most notably the head and hindquarters.

One troop favored blinding shows of red, white, and blue, while the other went in for equally intense displays of the same colors but in slightly altered proportions. As for the rest of the confrontation, it followed a predictable pattern as well. Alpha buffoons on one side would gesticulate dramatically, curl their lips in studied menace, roll their eyes in mocking scorn, and make loud grunting noises as the other side covered its own eyes and ears. Then the roles would be reversed.

Neither troop of buffoons appeared to tire of this performance, but after a while both would agree to withdraw and return for another dust-up in the future. And sure enough, there the two sides would soon be again, adopting the same threatening postures, making the same noises, and displaying the same brightly colored parts of their anatomy. It was enough to make one wonder whether they had changed their basic patterns of behavior at all since the rise of their species.

Or ever would.

THE MILK OF HUMAN KINDNESS

Once the milk of human kindness turned rancid.

The speed of the change was breathtaking. Neighbors who'd been on the best of terms for years were one day in each other's faces and the next day searching the Internet for guns and ammo.

When public opinion researchers asked the reason for this turnabout, the response never varied: "It's all about morals."

"Morals?" the researchers might then ask in order to gain a fuller sense of public thinking.

"Yeah, their sort don't have any!" a passerby might suddenly shout.

"What?" would come the equally loud response. "My sort don't have any? Just the only morality that counts, that's all!"

From that point on, crowds would rapidly gather and raise their own voices in supportive abuse. Regardless of the origin of any discord of this sort, it always deteriorated into charges that the other side was utterly immoral, as though this insult would deliver a death blow.

Instead of delivering a death blow, such charges merely prompted the opposing side to make wilder accusations that their hypocritical opponents presented themselves as having firm moral bearings when it was clear they had none whatsoever and weren't worth spitting on.

To hear these dueling insults, one might well think half the nation was convulsed with disgust for the other half, which felt much the same in return. And soon merely condemning your neighbor as the devil in disguise wasn't enough. Flying across the country to waive placards and hurl the same denunciation at perfect strangers on their own streets or in front of their own homes was deemed far more urgent, morality-wise.

The most rancorous dispute of all, it soon became clear, was over kindness to others as an essential component of moral thought and behavior. It wasn't merely that the two sides couldn't agree on a common definition of "kindness to others" or that the competing definitions seemed at times as far apart as possible. No, the true problem lay in the insistence by both sides that kindness itself must be seen as an eternal absolute: a universal ideal high above the messy complexities of real people striving to treat one another with dignity and good will each day.

It was vital to everybody involved in these ongoing quarrels to pre-serve this pure and eternal kindness with a capital "K" from being contaminated by the corrupted version of it being cynically advanced by the opposition. Who knew, each side screamed in turn, where such moral fuzziness by the other side was apt to lead? Nothing less than the moral health of the nation was at risk here. And that is how it came about that so many couldn't stomach the kindness of others anymore.

What would it take for people to replace Kindness that separated them with kindness that unified them again?

THE XENOPHOBE

Once a xenophobe turned up in the nation's blood supply.

Being a single-idea organism and thus extremely small, the xeno-phobe at first went undetected when transmitted from host to host to host, allowing it to multiply rapidly within each of its unwitting victims until its pernicious spread reached from one extremity to another and from the heart deep into the brain.

The initial indication that something might be amiss in a victim took the form of a mild but persistent fever. Then, in what seemed no time at all, the fever would grow more virulent and be accompanied by a steady swelling of the head. The sufferer began to have trouble seeing straight and typically spoke in a rambling or incoherent fashion. Subdued by paramedics one day while holding up traffic and threatening drivers if they didn't repeat faithfully some rambling tirade about "alien hordes," the hapless victim would be rushed to the nearest emergency room.

The prognosis was seldom good. By this point, the xenophobe would have so exploited every vulnerability of its now raving host that the prospects for a full return to good health seemed remote. Prone to fits of rage and addled paranoia, the sufferer often complicated matters by jerking free of all restraints and berating medical personnel who appeared in any way different or foreign. Shouts of "Get the hell away from me, you f****n' b*st**d!" and "Go back wherever you f****n' came from, b**ch!" were hurled in every direction, although the ranting could be rendered nearly unintelligible by a thick layer of foam covering the patient's mouth.

Then, just as suddenly as it had begun, the crisis might seem to pass. From being a hopeless case, convulsed by hysterical outbursts one moment and seemingly brain-dead the next, the sufferer would appear to be making a miraculous recovery. With astonishing speed, the fever broke, the paranoia faded, and the raving gibberish steadily gave way to more recognizable forms of expression. The victim returned home to open arms and resumed daily life as if nothing had happened.

Relatives, friends, and colleagues avoided any mention of the xenophobe attack, fearful of triggering a possible relapse. It was thought better to act as though the whole unpleasant episode amounted to no more than a false scare. In addition to sparing everybody any potential unpleasantness, this politic approach also allowed the community at large to feel reassured that the xenophobe was no longer of serious concern. By all appearances, its victim seemed fully cured.

So why not assume that all was well and just move on?

CHURCH AND STATE

Once Church and State hooked up at a singles bar.

They made for an unlikely couple, to be sure, seeming to have little if anything in common. Most who had even a passing acquaintance with the two would have been surprised to find either of them in the type of meat market where they met. Hardly "swingers" in anybody's book, both Church and State had a reputation for preferring the company of those they already knew and for feeling uncomfortable with any notion of risking potentially dangerous liaisons with strangers.

That might have been the way things remained had it not been for the uninvited urging of certain friends who fancied themselves matchmakers and thought the reserved pair just needed a helpful nudge to "overcome their inhibitions and expand their horizons," as these friends put it with a wink and a nod. What a waste if the two didn't venture out and discover how much excitement a little mixing might bring to their lives.

Arriving at the singles bar at roughly the same time, the self-appointed cupids who formed the respective retinues of Church and State quickly set about executing various schemes to maneuver the two into closer proximity and keep their glasses filled. There were plenty of awkward moments at first, but as familiarity grew and things began to loosen up, the pair might be seen to touch pinkies furtively from time to time as though by accident, then to lean together ever so gently and then more unblushingly as their last inhibitions faded until, unable to keep their hands off each other, they drawled incoherently and groped away for all they were worth.

Confident they'd accomplished their mission, the matchmaking friends on both sides quietly withdrew and went home to sleep off the effects of the evening. Not so for the blotto pair of Church and State, however, who had to be shown the bar's door at closing time. As they staggered away locked in an ungainly embrace, little of what the two could be heard to mumble made much sense.

At most, it sounded like a rambling difference of opinion over whose place to head for and who should be on top and who on the bottom once they got there.

THE GARDEN GNOMES

Once a gang of garden gnomes seized control of a grand estate.

Being gnomes, they benefited from the fact that nobody had taken them very seriously during the time they spent planning their audacious caper. They'd seemed, when notice was taken of them at all, to be simply a collection of comical trolls that might raise an occasional smile but little more.

How they actually managed to pull off their takeover was a matter of considerable puzzlement, but once in control, they acted as if they'd been destined from the start to find themselves in the position they now were.

What could be said for certain about the takeover was that it happened while those who owned the estate and who might have been presumed to have some interest in safeguarding what had been bequeathed to them over generations were napping in broad daylight.

After their triumph, the gnomes' primary concern was to make themselves appear more commanding in stature by whatever means it took. They were led in this effort by one of their number, a boastful figure nicknamed "Greatest Gnome Ever" because he was given to calling himself that nearly every time he opened his mouth.

Besides trying out various makeshift stilts to increase their own stature (an expedient that produced at best a dangerous staggering about and not a few unfortunate mishaps), the other gnomes spent most of their time puffing themselves up and striking poses in front of each other in hopes of finding one that made them look stately. This also proved more difficult than expected, though, because none of them demonstrated they had any idea how a "stately garden gnome" might look and behave.

So they settled on telling themselves that all those who might try to take the estate back were actually smaller than they were. How it was possible to be smaller than they were took some imagining, of course.

Eventually the gnomes just declared in unison, "To heck with worrying about stature and appearance!" and got down to business. The business they got down to was selling off most of the estate as quickly as possible to the highest bidders. By unloading whatever they themselves saw no use for, they could reduce their responsibilities to a minimum and have more time for the leisure activities, such as miniature golf, to which they were better suited by temperament and experience.

Here again, they were led by "Greatest Gnome Ever," who had taken up the practice of swinging away at anything and everything as a restful break from the weighty burdens of leadership. Besides, stories of chopping down cherry trees and splitting rails were already legendary in the history of the estate, he announced to his minions. And since his own achievements would be greater and more noteworthy than those of the past by far, why shouldn't theirs be as well?

In this spirit the entire group of gnomes took up little axes and pledged to chop and split things up themselves to demonstrate their loyalty to "Greatest Gnome Ever." The trouble was, with so much of the estate having been sold off by this point, there wasn't a great deal left for them to set their sights on. Nevertheless, their great leader sent them marching out every morning, led by his favorites, named Sleazy #1, Sleazy #2 Sleazy #3, Sleazy #4, and so forth, all whistling a happy tune and keeping an eye open for anything left standing to take a whack at.

Once even these targets were gone, the gnomes barely paused in their whistling before they shifted their attention to the majestic white mansion that stood at the heart of the estate, urged on as always by "Greatest Gnome Ever," who now insisted on also being called "Chopper in Chief." There was enough in the mansion to keep them all swinging away for a while at least.

They began with the furniture, which had proved too big for them in any case.

THE CANTIPEDE

Once a cantipede was hired as the press secretary for a prominent but erratic politician.

The cantipede appeared better qualified for the job than the politician's previous press secretaries. To begin with, "cant" was part of its name, so it was naturally assumed the cantipede shouldn't have much difficulty taking up its duties from day one. More important, though, was its remarkable flexibility. The cantipede possessed more than enough legs to move in whatever direction was called for when a shift in the thinking or intent of its boss needed to be explained to the public. If it had to shift this way or that, it obediently hastened to do so. And if it suddenly had to backtrack, back it would hustle as though it hadn't taken a single step in any other direction. So suited was the cantipede to being this particular politician's press secretary, in fact, that soon it was difficult to think of one without immediately thinking of the other as well.

Then one day the cantipede began inexplicably tripping over its own feet. These mishaps weren't much of a hindrance at first. And as long as they were minor, a false step or two could be covered up well enough by merely shifting from one leg to several others in a sort of improvised skipping in place, a move that might even be taken for having been part of the plan.

If truth be told, however, it was not part of the plan, and this fact caused the cantipede increasing concern. If it proved unable to keep up with the pace at which it was being asked to change direction all the time, how long would it be before it was replaced by another press secretary who could manage a more convincing display of fancy footwork regardless of the dodging about required?

The cantipede thought long and hard and came up with an offense it felt would be the best defense against being summarily sacked. It looked to its strength: legs. It just needed more of them. So each time its boss changed direction, the cantipede dutifully tried to sprout a few new legs to help it follow suit step for step.

Initially, the strategy worked well enough, although this generating of new legs to stand on was sometimes a challenge, especially when the signals the cantipede received weren't in themselves easy to follow.

But it did manage, after a fashion, to produce whatever legs were needed to match shifting thoughts from the boss, looking in the process a bit like Athena struggling to emerge feet first from the head of a befuddled Zeus.

It goes without saying that adding legs on demand has its risks, and eventually these were bound to overtake the cantipede. Presented with its frantic efforts, reporters became ever less certain exactly what direction the hapless, put-upon press secretary was headed in, whether forward or backward, to the right or to the left. Some days, the flustered cantipede appeared to be trying to move in all directions at once in a flurry of contradictory thrashings about. Other days, it seemed merely to be running in circles while insisting it was always on the straight and narrow.

Not surprisingly, there were moments during its breathtaking contortions when the cantipede was in obvious danger of falling flat on its face. More generally, it waged a ceaseless struggle just to keep its head clear of its multiplying legs as it peeped out from their thick blur with a look of desperation. There must be a better way of presenting to the press and public a prominent but erratic politician's shifts in thinking, the loyal cantipede often muttered to itself.

A way with less chance of being struck so often in the mouth by its own flailing feet.

THE GORILLA

Once an 800-pound gorilla wondered if it should go on a diet.

It had similar thoughts every time it found itself having to press against the wall at receptions in the nation's capital so more of the usual invitees could crowd in.

Anyone the gorilla ever asked about the matter, though, answered, "You can't be serious! Diets are for those who should have learned a little restraint long ago."

"I just thought my presence might be a bother to some at times like this."

"My dear friend, have you ever heard anybody at these gatherings voice the slightest concern about your presence? You shouldn't be so sensitive. Now, if you don't mind, I see a congressional aide over there I need to have a quick word with."

Was it in fact too sensitive, the gorilla asked itself? Or was the comment just a tactful way of hiding the awkward reality that other guests regularly chose to pretend it wasn't there?

"A penny for your thoughts?"

"I beg your pardon," the gorilla answered with a start, looking down at a new face looking up into its own.

"A penny for your thoughts. You seemed like you had something you wanted to get off your chest. Though who'd hear you over all this noise, eh? Somebody should blow a whistle every now and then just to give people a break from all the glad-handing and backslapping and a chance to get their glasses refilled or to reach for more canapés."

"Why don't you blow a whistle?" the gorilla responded.

"Never thought anybody'd pay attention. Now, I'll wager you could get their attention if you wanted to, an 800-pound gorilla like you."

"Tell me, do I look overweight?"

"Aren't you supposed to be this big?"

The gorilla wasn't sure whether the question was genuine or a joke. Nonplussed, it excused itself and began to head for a set of large glass doors onto the terrace, edging gingerly through the press of lobbyists turned public servants and public servants turned lobbyists, military contractors with military brass in tow, corporate donors with a

favor to ask, industry lawyers and government regulators, special interest fundraisers, off-shore accountants, and so many others now filling
the room elbow to elbow and wall to wall.

"Excuse me . . . sorry . . . forgive me . . . so sorry . . . excuse me . .
. ," the gorilla mumbled as it squeezed past, fearing to offend.

When it finally reached the terrace doors, the gorilla labored to
open them and slip out into the evening air. There it found rows of
chairs apparently moved outside to make room for more and more
reception guests. And on many of the chairs sat other gorillas, some
much larger than it, and all staring off silently into space.

All wondering too, perhaps, if their size was ever considered a
bother by anyone inside?

VII

THE IMMORTAL

Once an immortal decided to call it quits.

When so many mortals hoped to enjoy eternal bliss after they died, this immortal's embrace of the reverse might seem baffling.

The death option certainly didn't appeal to other immortals, who were none too pleased to be told their entire reason for existing might have less to recommend it than they thought. It was—or so this bothersome malcontent in their midst claimed—devoid of any recognition that existence might offer something other than endless repetitions of the known and a tedious search for time-killing diversions to lessen the ennui of living forever.

What was the attraction of such arid monotony, the renegade immortal asked again and again. Where was the thirst anymore for experiences that suddenly upended everything you'd come to assume about yourself and replaced those assumptions with a fresh start offered by the unpredictable? Even the fleeting lives of mortals looked attractive by comparison with a divine existence that had about as much thrill left to it as eternally flossing one's teeth in the mirror.

At least there were alluring possibilities still in what mortals faced. Nothing was ever finished, no matter how "complete" or "perfect" they naively declared it to be. Their blindness to the potential value of the unfinished over the completed and of imperfection over perfection was what made so many humans endearing. Constantly flogging themselves to accomplish "something for the ages" and then flogging themselves again with worries they might not succeed—how these mere mortals stirred one's sympathies, what with all they had left still to learn! Masterpieces, legacies, honor, conquest, trophies and prizes and records of every sort, fortune and fame regardless of how these were won, position and privilege and all—humans strove so hard for so little, such trifles in the end, that the renegade immortal couldn't help but be touched by their endless myopia.

When right there before them were spread more reasons to marvel than they ever dreamed of: all the taints, scars, lapses, errors, and defects that made their lives the constant gamble they were. Full of uncertain promise and vulnerability, no wonder mortals were so fascinating in ways no immortal could claim to be. For who among those spared from ever having to come to terms with their own death could understand the doomed hope which humans gripped more fiercely each day they neared their ultimate defeat?

In the end, this tragic hope had a nobility that outweighed everything else and should leave even gods in speechless awe.

THE MISANTHROPE

Once reports came in that a misanthrope had been spotted on the outskirts of town.

This news caused quite a stir, but serious doubts about the sighting were raised almost at once. Most in dispute was whether the being in question belonged to the species of true misanthropes or was, on the contrary, an example of that rarely seen relative, the mock (sometimes referred to as the "pseudo") misanthrope. This second species, having diverged in its development from the true misanthrope at some point in the past, was known to compete for the same habitat but had been steadily losing ground when it came to the survival of the fittest among misanthropes.

Simply stated, the mock misanthrope had clung stubbornly to an approach to life's challenges that true misanthropes no longer fully embraced or had abandoned outright: a reliance upon the contents of one's own braincase to make it from one day to the next. In fact, to trust in anything other than the intelligence of the species struck the mock misanthrope as a grievous lack of faith in oneself and one's kind. Any neglect of these inherited mental strengths in favor of some makeshift and tenuous survival ploy would send it into a frustrated protest. "What are we," it might shout at such times, "an evolutionary dead end? A waste of good gray matter?"

Unfortunately, rather than encouraging others to make better use of what gray matter they did in fact possess, these sarcastic barbs only drew attention to the mock misanthrope itself, with the negative consequences that might be expected. Its criticisms typically met with hostile silence or else a grumbling dismissal and an avoidance of further contact. Little wonder, then, that the mock misanthrope was in trouble and was spotted with increasing rarity. There was even talk of the need to place it on the endangered species list.

By contrast, the survival strategy of the other branch on the misanthropes' evolutionary tree had demonstrated clear advantages time and again. The true misanthrope decided at an early stage in its development that relying on one's own wits and strengths alone could be suicidal. These might fall so far short of what was required to advance one's individual prospects and those of the species as a whole that abandoning them as often and as fully as necessary became the preferred course.

With the stakes so high, no alternative to risky self-reliance should be overlooked. The most common tactic adopted by the true misanthrope whenever danger arose was to hope for some miracle of deliverance or pity by powers greater than oneself. Lacking confidence in itself when faced with any imminent threat, it perfected the art of making itself appear as small as possible and therefore not worth the trouble of putting an end to. It might be heard to plead at such times, "O, what a weak and worthless wretch am I! Have mercy on me for my miserable failings!"

After repeating this trusted formula until it was hoarse, the true misanthrope would slowly open one eye and look anxiously about. If nothing had happened, the true misanthrope would take this as a sign it must be doing something right and resolve to make itself appear even smaller and confess its weaknesses even more plaintively next time, if that's what circumstances called for. Counting too much on your own ability to meet life's challenges simply wasn't a safe calculation and might even land you in deeper trouble for your pains. Better to lament your shortcomings loudly instead and turn your fate over to some superior being, then hope for the best.

An alternative survival strategy that might be resorted to by the true misanthrope was to veer to the opposite extreme, noisily drawing attention to itself by claiming its species represented perfection and thus was too important not to leave a gaping hole in creation if ever eliminated from it. To support such a declaration, the true misanthrope would set up an idealized version of itself on a grand pedestal, declare it the measure of all things, then worship it day and night as transcending every limitation of nature and time.

If the former tactic of self-denigration sought to arouse the pity of an almighty power as a way of deflecting any threat, real or imagined, this second tactic aimed at feeding an absolute conviction that the species would remain forever at the apex of existence through its intrinsic strength and beauty. To both of these tactics, the mock misanthrope would rejoin, "Why not just be who you are, right here and right now, without cringing or boasting? Have faith in yourself, draw courage from yourself, whatever happens. Answer the challenge within to live out your own meaning and do justice to it. Celebrate the best in yourself, the best in humanity. And if you must bow down in worship, bow down to those who have such faith in the species that they'd sacrifice themselves for the sake of total strangers."

As natural selection took its course, the species of misanthrope possessing the adaptive trait of alternating between self-doubt and self-glorification multiplied rapidly and spread around the globe. Specimens could be found everywhere, enjoying the considerable fruits of either deflating or puffing themselves up as two halves of the same survival strategy: one that forced the increasingly outnumbered mock misanthropes, with only themselves to count on, ever closer and closer to dying out. In light of this fact, it was ultimately the consensus among experts that the particular misanthrope reportedly seen near the city limits was almost certainly not of the endangered mock variety.

It must instead have been one of the far more common true misanthropes.

THE BEDBUG

Once a bedbug thought it had "found god."

Admittedly, the bedbug, being very small, was only hazarding a guess about the colossal form that rolled and sweated and scratched itself night after night in the sheets they shared. But since it was so much bigger than the bedbug, how could it be anything else?

Whatever this enormous being was, it certainly seemed generous, for it gave every indication of knowing exactly when the bedbug was most in need of it. Absent for long periods of time, it would suddenly reappear just when the bedbug had grown so weak with waiting that it feared the worst.

And when the bedbug's god finally did return, the long absence was quickly forgotten in thankful rejoicing. In no time at all, a re-newed sense of well-being filled the bedbug, replacing its recent anxie-ty with elation. "Mine! Mine! This god is mine all mine alone!" it would repeat for hours on end, counting itself blessed above all other bedbugs on earth.

Satisfied with its lot once more, freed from worries about mere survival, the bedbug had time to reflect further on the nature of its benefactor. What exactly was this extraordinary being that appeared and disappeared at will and without whom the bedbug wondered what would become of its own existence really like? Where did it go when it disappeared, or was it actually still around even when it seemed to be absent, watching the bedbug languish in wait? And how could its evi-dent generosity to the bedbug be reconciled with the fact that often it would seize a neighboring bug with lightning quickness and squash it flat?

In truth, the bedbug had no way of grasping the real nature of the colossus it had come to depend upon. The difference in size was simp-ly too great; the bedbug was as nothing by comparison. That was the extent of what it thought it knew for certain. The rest was pure specu-lation. The only way the bedbug found to conceive of this great being, the only way to give it some imagined form as a focus for the bedbug's humble gratitude, was to picture the mysterious benefactor in its own image: as an immense, all-powerful version of itself.

Even this wasn't easy to manage, though, especially on those occasions when the great being would return after a long absence accompanied by a second great being, with whom it rolled about in the bed like booming thunder. On these occasions, the bedbug just had to accept that some things were beyond its comprehending. The safest course to take in the face of the inexplicable was simply to count your blessings wherever you could find them.

And on that basis, weren't two gods even better than one?

THE POTATOES

Once a potato thought it heard a voice.

Not just any voice. The voice of a child, to be more exact, arguing with itself over where on the potato to attach an outsized plastic ear.

The pain already visited upon the potato by the sharp jab of a single spike-tipped ear was bad enough, but when its tormentor must have decided a second ear was necessary and now tried one clumsy thrust after another to secure it in some wished-for relationship of absolute balance with the first, the pain was multiplied many times over. After which came a nose planted between the two ears, then one eye and nearby another.

Where each new feature ended up suggested a master plan not too well thought through or else settled on by default when patience ran out. "There, that'll do" must have been the decision ultimately arrived at, followed by a giggle of delight at the effect produced. That giggle caused the greatest pain. Straining to focus its eyes as the child turned away in search of the next cartoonish bit of plastic to jam into it, the potato struggled to understand what could possibly be going on in a mind that would take pleasure in such mistreatment.

Only when it felt the gashing thrust of a pair of lips did the potato find itself blurting out from hitherto unsuspected depths within the words "Why are you doing this to me?" At first, the child only giggled some more, as though its own pleasure was justification enough, before leaning over to pick up a second potato and bring it close to the first.

"Man potato, meet woman potato. Woman potato, meet man potato. Good? Good? Happy? Happy?"

What a woeful sight! The potato could hardly bear what it beheld. The same seemed true for the other potato, judging by its equal anguish at what it saw.

How like a willful child to believe the innate attractions of a potato could be improved upon. For in place of the wonder to be found in a splendid tuber fresh from the soil—the full richness of life in all its swellings and presence—these deforming wounds visited upon the potato pair betrayed the brutality of an arbitrary perfection. To judge by the repeated efforts at fixing ears, eyes, noses, lips and whatever else was to come in just the right places, the goal must have been some rigid combination of absolute symmetry, regularity, completeness, and permanence as a universal standard of beauty. Quite a lot to demand of a potato.

But far less, in fact, than what the merest spud attained without any guidance or model whatsoever.

Such a mismatch between reality and wish fulfillment in forging an ideal beauty was bound to have unwelcome results. And when these became obvious, the child's disappointment quickly turned to frustration and from frustration to a wailing attack upon the objects of its mounting ire.

"Ugly man potato! Ugly woman potato! Bad! Bad! Bad!" the child raged, ultimately hurling both to the floor and kicking them around and around.

THE FOXHOUND

Once a foxhound began to have second thoughts about chasing foxes.

This unaccustomed frame of mind brought on little more than a mild uneasiness at first: on a par, perhaps, with momentarily losing sight of a reddish phantom in the morning fog like any of those that had for years led the foxhound and its baying kennelmates on a chase across damp, uneven ground. Such a vague disquiet was also hard to distinguish from the kind of light woozy spell that might come over the hound at the end of a long pursuit and then pass without further effect. A little rest, typically, and all would be right with the foxhound's world again.

Except that it wasn't anymore. These and other strange new feelings did not fade as expected. Instead, they lasted a bit longer after each hunt in a rising anxiety that came and went on its own, like a taunting fox pacing back and forth in full view right outside the kennel fence.

Despite all the thrills of past hunts and all the praise still earned from the master of hounds, the passion for running a fox to ground was plainly lessening as this unwelcome state of mind deepened. Once so compelling it seemed the very reason for being born a foxhound, rushing pell-mell across field and stream in pursuit of the prey was now taking on the dogtrot of custom or of merely going through the motions so as not to draw the attention of its keepers. Or the notice as well of its fellow foxhounds, none of whom seemed troubled by any queasy feelings.

On the contrary, their eyes narrowed with disbelief when it mentioned its bafflement. Some eyes even to cold slits of suspicion. What caused this flagging commitment to ridding the world of foxes, its companions demanded to know. The critters were as shifty and dangerous as ever, were they not? Their sly nature would never change, and any slacking off in pursuing them, any hesitation to join in pulling a fox from its lair and tearing it limb from limb, was a sign of weakness that would surely be noted beyond the kennel. And the next time the hunting horns sounded, what then?

The foxhound was reminded in no uncertain terms that not only its own wellbeing but the wellbeing of all its comrades depended upon flawless teamwork in the cornering of foxes. How long would fox-hounds be housed and fed, did it suppose, if they didn't prove themselves worthy of that sought-after pat on the head for their unfailing dedication? Had they deserved the rewards of their domestication or not?

One pace slower or one chorus of barking compliance less and questions about their trustworthiness would certainly arise. Once that happened, where would any of them be? Think of the pack, the foxhound was urged. And if that wasn't enough, think of itself. Without the hunt, what separated a foxhound from a fox ultimately? Answer that!

The foxhound realized it had no ready answer to such questions, particularly the last one, which carried the weight of a direct command to give an accounting of itself. What did separate a foxhound from a fox? In truth, mistaking the fox for a small dog or a standard hunting dog for a large fox might conceivably happen. But there must be ways to distinguish them under the skin. Qualities that made plain any fox-hound's superiority to foxes.

In its state of mounting frustration, however, the foxhound wasn't sure it could name these distinguishing qualities with the confidence it once had enjoyed. In what ways was it more than just an oversized version of a fox? There remained that old assurance of being "man's best friend," of course. That ought to count for something after thousands of years of dogs heeling to a master's slightest wish.

And what of the foxhound's sense of discipline: the steady response to every test of its intelligence and its devotion to task? These had to count in the larger view as being worthy of admiration, more so at least than a fox's brute instinct and cunning. If not, if it and the fox were merely on a par, coequals facing one another across a divide between self-discipline and utter wildness, what reason would there have been for striving so diligently to overcome the savage state? Sacrifice must have its demonstrable proofs and rewards, mustn't it?

Yet these longed-for reassurances of worth might not turn out to be as telling as a hound would wish. And the more this one wrestled with the questions before it, the more its failure to answer any of them haunted the wait between hunts. At first the lack of certainty had troubled only its morning hours, fading as these gave way to the traditional safeguards of daily life within the kennel fence. But that release from misgivings grew shorter and shorter, until even the pleasures of a bone to gnaw or a full bowl at mealtime could not quiet the doubts that threatened to push the foxhound to total distraction.

There were even times now when it would fall victim to sudden blackouts and come to with its nose against the inside of the fence, trembling in alarm. Would it soon be in danger of losing control of its life altogether and spending the rest of it harried by self-distrust? Perhaps tempted in a fit of madness to burrow under the fence and be off, abandoning everything that had given it stability and direction?

And all the while, the question of what separated the foxhound from a fox refused to go away. The dividing line between it and this feral creature rose into view only to fade away again, then reappear somewhere else and vanish just as completely, like hedgerows on the landscape of dreams. Until the only release the foxhound felt might offer any hope whatsoever was the total destruction of this menace to its sense of being and self-worth. So it seized upon what suddenly seemed obvious: every fox for miles around must die. Must die!

From that day on, not a hunt took place without the foxhound's pushing itself into the lead, running like it was possessed and bent on being the first to overtake the prey. No obstacle could slow it and no distance make it give up the chase. With the stakes being its life or the fox's (nothing less than the loss of meaning to its very existence or the salvaging of it through unflagging resolve), was it any wonder that when it finally brought a fox to bay, no mercy held the foxhound back?

Not the slightest hesitation at ridding its world, once and for all, of this tormenting reminder of the untamed life.

THE BEAST-WITHIN

Once a beast-within spent a great deal of time licking its wounds.

That wasn't surprising, for it had suffered one wound after another over the years. The life of a beast-within struck it at times like a walk through a bramble patch. On all sides were sharp threats that tore at the skin and brought fresh pain to the surface.

This pain the beast-within nursed in private for the most part. Experience had taught it there were fewer complications that way, at least in one's day-to-day contacts with the outside world. You had to be careful not to reveal too much of the inner you or to expect too much sympathy from others. They had their own secrets to shield from sight.

The beast-within could tell this was the case as it rode the 6:15 express into the city each morning. All of the seats were occupied by outwardly self-confident riders reading their newspapers or checking their email accounts before they reached their destinations. To look at them, you'd never guess they'd spent the night struggling with their own beast-within or were still trying to hide the telltale evidence of that struggle before the train came to a stop.

Strange, that after all this time, people still fought so hard to vanquish or simply repudiate the faithful companion that had stood by them through thick and thin and had in return received nothing but ingratitude.

Their beast-within was always there when they needed its help with some detour from the path of virtue, some depravity or cruelty or betrayal that might have to be denied or explained away later. As recognition of that devotion, it only asked for the merest sign of thankfulness.

Yet what did it actually receive? Whenever things went wrong, who got the sticks and stones? Instead of doing the right thing, instead of standing by their beast-within and taking on at least part of the blame, those who'd been more than happy to benefit from its selfless fidelity invariably sought to distance themselves from it.

They turned away as from a pariah, cursing it and accusing it of having tricked them into "regrettable lapses." Soon they'd convinced themselves it was their beast-within that was to blame for every misstep they'd ever made. Casting the full guilt upon it, they sought forgiveness for themselves alone, pledging to shun it forevermore. Was it any surprise then that their beast-within felt betrayed and lashed back in aggrieved self-defense? In its view, it had only acted out of obedience to their deepest desires.

The results of this painful strife were predictable. The commuter train was full of them: seemingly composed, lifetime pass holders who were inwardly counting the wounds they'd given and received, feeling themselves deeply wronged and wishing they could creep away somewhere to lick clean the worst of what they'd suffered.

For it was, without doubt, a wound-licking age.

THE BEAR

Once a bear attracted quite a following in faith-based wrestling.

It wasn't a case of a bear's retiring from the ring and then taking up religion, as occasionally happens. This one was still at the height of its career. No, this bear was simply the first to recognize a role for wrestling in big-time religion.

It all began one night in a sold-out arena, after the bear, cheered on by screaming fans, had squeezed an opponent's ribs until they gave way. The bear looked out into the spotlight-threaded darkness as it dropped its limp foe and had an epiphany.

These multitudes hungered for something, it realized. That was why they showed up night after night, city after city. They gathered together in search of something to believe in and dedicate themselves to.

And then the bear had its second epiphany of the night. What the screaming crowd really sought was something to hold onto in confusing times. Outside the ropes, in the chaotic world of life's uncertainties, telling right from wrong was tricky. But inside the ropes, the smash-mouth struggle between good and evil was easier to follow.

Seized with this recognition, the bear stepped over its now unconscious opponent, grabbed the ringside announcer's microphone, and began to shout in all directions.

"Listen to me! Listen to me, all of you out there! I know what you're looking for! I know what you need!"

Members of the crowd rose to their feet as one, uncertain what to expect but ready for anything.

"You want the Match of Matches! You want the Final Showdown!"

The crowd burst into deafening agreement.

Drawing in a deep breath, the bear then turned to the nearest television camera and issued the biggest challenge of its career: "If you're out there, Prince of Darkness . . . if you're out there . . . listen up!"

The crowd went wild. Shouts of "Prince of Darkness! Prince of Darkness!" boomed through the air.

"Oh, you can call yourself 'The Wily One,' or you can call yourself 'The Archfiend,' and you may think you can't be whupped," the bear continued. "But I got news for ya! Armageddon's comin'!"

"Armageddon's comin'! Armageddon's comin'! Bring it on! Bring it on!"

"I dare you to meet me, no holds barred, next month at 'Doomsday in Dallas'!"

"Doomsday! Doomsday!" The chant rang around the arena as the bear, pumping its paws defiantly overhead, stalked down the aisle to the showers.

Later, however, as "Doomsday in Dallas" approached with no response from the Prince of Darkness, the bear began to wonder if it should have put a little more oomph into the challenge. Was it a bit flat? It sounded good each night the bear repeated it in venues large and small, but were the Armageddon taunts strong enough to draw the Devil out? What if he didn't show up?

Conversely, what if the Devil did show up but refused to go down for the count? It would be absolutely in character for Satan not to take a choreographed fall. Then again, suppose he did take the fall but then walked away without signing up for the expected pay-per-view rematch? And what would that do to ticket sales and crowd numbers thereafter? How do you hold your audience share after Doomsday's come and gone without anything happening?

This was serious. Religious wrestling, the bear realized, needed the Devil far more than the Devil needed it.

THE BULLFROG

Once a bullfrog was looked to by many who sought a spiritual master.

Drawn by word of the bullfrog's sonorous croak and serene pose as it sat on a lily pad surveying an old pond from beneath lowered eyelids, large crowds showed up to line the banks of the pond, adopt what they took to be a frog squat, and squint soulfully back in the bullfrog's direction. The only time they shifted their gaze was to assure themselves that nobody around them had a more committed squat or more soulful squint.

Although quite a few were able to manage one or both of these after a fashion, none had the confidence to attempt the bullfrog's awe-inspiring croak. Instead, they concentrated on counting the number of times it blinked per minute and attributed great significance to that number, depending upon whether it was odd or even. Differences of opinion in this regard could, and often did, result in disdainful glances being cast about and sometimes even under-the-breath denunciations of insufficient effort by others.

Whenever the bullfrog shot out its tongue and snatched something from the air, it noticed that a number of the more earnest members of the crowd attempted to follow its lead. They looked exceedingly awkward in their efforts, the bullfrog thought, wondering how many of them actually managed to catch anything in the end. Out of curiosity, the bullfrog asked those nearest to it whether they were enjoying the tranquility of the pond.

"The pond?"

"Yes, this old pond. Isn't that why you came here?"

"No. We came here because we are seekers."

"Oh? And what is it you are seeking?"

"Enlightened guidance. Ultimate understanding. We've come to learn the secret of your matchless croak."

"It's just a croak, you realize."

"Ah, but we know it is much, much more."

"Really? What is it, then?"

"That is what we've come here to learn from you."

At that instant and without warning, the bullfrog leaped into the pond. The sound of water startled the throng lining the banks. Many thought to follow the bullfrog's example and throw themselves into the pond, were it not for fear they might come down with a rash from doing so. Others favored waiting for the bullfrog to resurface and perhaps instruct them on how to interpret what had just happened. The bullfrog did resurface, but at some distance and with only its eyes protruding above the water, unnoticed by all.

As time passed without anything further happening, the crowds began to grow restless and then to break up and drift away. The prevailing mood was one of disappointment, of having been let down in their spiritual aspirations by the bullfrog. Even those who had thrown themselves into the pond in solemn imitation of it, not once but two or three or four times running, began to feel they might have been mistaken, possibly deceived. Most importantly, everyone was convinced they'd lost precious time in their search for ultimate understanding.

The bullfrog was clearly not spiritual-master material, as far as they were concerned.

VIII

THE POSSUM

Once a possum came to realize how difficult it is to appear dim.

It wasn't enough to move slowly and look dopey much of the time. The possum's mastery of the night was well known and prompted not a few acquaintances to lament the fact that it didn't show more of its mental dexterity in the daylight hours as well.

"Think of the brilliant career you could have if you just applied yourself more," it was regularly urged.

"Now, why would I want what so many call a 'brilliant career'?" the possum just as regularly responded with a yawn.

"What a question! Wasting abilities like yours, nobody should do that."

"Nobody?" asked the possum with another, widening yawn.

"Nobody who's interested in leaving a mark on the world."

The possum closed one eye and then the other, as though forcing itself to take on an unwelcome task, and inquired, "What mark might that be?"

"Why, some proof you've counted in the eyes of the world, that you aren't simply an anonymous onlooker when it comes to the grand march of history."

"Would that be so bad? Being an anonymous onlooker?"

"If the slightest effort could bring you fame and fortune, it certainly is. Think of the reputation you'd gain and the money you could make from best-selling books and inspirational lectures about nearly anything at all these days!"

"Fame and fortune, those should be my goals?"

"'When in Rome . . .'"

Waiting for the possum to complete the well-known maxim, some of these advice givers checked their watches and others wondered if it hadn't in fact drifted off to sleep. Unaccustomed to being ignored like this, they turned to addressing one another directly in voices they trusted were loud enough to rouse the possum from even the deepest slumber.

"Isn't it a shame to see such utter lack of ambition?"

"Especially when the avenues to success are so wide open."

"With virtually no effort at all and with the right connections, one can rise to positions of great influence and prestige in today's society."

"But what do you have to sacrifice in the process?" the possum murmured, taking the speakers by surprise.

"Surely it's worth sacrificing, whatever it is."

"Including your peace of mind?"

"Come, come, you exaggerate. And even if you didn't exaggerate, take a pragmatic, real-world view. Only a fool would hide the mental capabilities you were born with, when merely appearing to be smart could be all that's required!"

"Appearing to be smart is easy," the possum sighed, opening both eyes slowly. "It's actually being smart that is hard. But being 'foolish' when so many others claim to be in the know, now that's harder still. Much harder."

THE SUNFLOWER

Once a sunflower lost its bearings during a solar eclipse.

Or to be more precise, it lost the guiding reassurance of time. Nothing like this had happened to the sunflower before. Not only was it subtly attuned to the advance of the sun each day but it also had total recall of the moment when any past experience in its life had occurred, as well as the moments just before and after.

The sunflower had anticipated the same would be true of every moment to come through the rest of the summer and well into autumn. All was predictable, hour to hour, day to day, week to week, month to month.

And then the sun went out. Not all at once, but gradually, which made its disappearance even more alarming. Sudden darkness would have been easier to deal with. If the sunflower's ordered world came to an end in an abrupt cataclysm, well, what could you do? Things just hadn't worked out.

But this extended fading of the light, this deepening uncertainty, was an agonizing affair. One had time to lament the slow disappearance of one's entire world into shadow. And with it the extinguishing of each memory or expectation that world had produced. Past, present, future—all vanishing together.

With the sun gone, the flower began to sense the troubling contours of an existence it had never dreamed of in the light of day. It found the change thoroughly disorienting and suffered, amid the shifting and vague shapes, a rush of vertigo. There was no rhyme or reason to count on, no reassuring lines running straight to the horizon and joining there against confusion. The sunflower couldn't even be certain of its companions in the field around it, only that they, too, likely turned and turned about unsteadily in the gloom.

Soon, however, an unexpected calm began to settle out of that gloom.

No, calm wasn't the word for it, the sunflower soon realized. More like hushed fascination. In the depths of the eclipse, when nothing was as it always had been, the possibility that the sunflower's world might stay like this left it wavering between a wish for the sun's return and a strange reluctance to have it reappear.

The sunflower tried to imagine what life might be like in perpetual darkness. Without the accustomed bearings, it could be anything. As if the sunflower were the first on earth, setting its face towards the unknown with all the hazard of a life gamble. Nothing taken for certain nor rejected yet. Free as no flower had ever been free, bearing the seeds of a present without past or future. Ready to live for the moment alone.

But then, from behind the great dark promise of the moon, the sun began to reclaim the sky.

THE SARDINE

Once a sardine was feeling kind of lonesome.

That hadn't always been the case. Precisely the opposite emotion had characterized most of the sardine's life, in fact. Rather than seeking the closeness of other sardines, it had felt uncomfortable being pressed on all sides by those with whom it felt it shared little.

Not that it nursed any illusions it wasn't a sardine like the rest of its species. Darting about together in frenzied bait balls, it and all the others might appear identical in every regard. But this sardine had long been convinced such likeness was not the full story. As far as it could tell, few of those around it experienced the same doubt it did regarding the common assumption that all sardines could be defined by what they shared. How many times had others' unquestioned confidence that it swam in the same waters they did troubled its peace of mind: their chummy claim that "we're all in this together" repeated over and over throughout the bait ball as if this assurance were an undeniable plus and its value beyond debate?

To which "No, thank you" had been the only response the sardine ever felt was honest. Going it alone, indifferent to the dangers, had been its wish always. And it didn't matter that "going it alone" might not have amounted at first to more than straying a short distance every now and then from the swirling mass. The sardine's imagination extended those few moments of independence to a lifetime far below the surface comfort of others' company, down, down where nightmarish creatures carried their own lights and savaged one another.

In the depths of the sardine's awareness lay another life that the frenzy of the bait ball held at bay only by shutting out anything that distracted its members from their frantic veering about amid perceived threats. As though each abrupt shift wasn't simply a repeated and desperate pursuit of mere survival.

The futility of this compulsive drive here and there to no lasting gain was clear to see from outside the bait ball. Carried along by the force of the dizzying angst that bound all sardines together (constantly worried about turning one way while their companions turned another), little wonder all eyes were directed towards any sardine that claimed to know where it was going and could provide the lead others gratefully followed. Until directions changed, that was. Yet when this inevitably happened, the assumption that all sardines should now follow a new leader never wavered. So the entire school was off again in a flash, as though they'd never been headed anywhere else than they now were.

From the outside looking in, the sardine had concluded, at least there was no blind confidence that life as a sardine was anything more than an iffy proposition. You were doubtless better off on your own, whatever the increased risks. Following your own direction within the bait ball was impossible. Following it outside could leave you prey to horrors from the deep, there was no denying that, but the risk was worth taking. Without the prospect of endless reaches to explore, what was "ocean" supposed to mean?

So why did life as a sardine apart leave this one occasionally longing again for the press of the crowd? Was it really prepared to trade struggles of its own choosing for those set by round after narrowing round of reflexive dodges for safety until the limits of one's life were not much greater in the end than a small metal tin?

No, it wasn't the expectation of safety in numbers that caused the sardine to feel the renewed draw of the bait ball at such times. What, return in hopes the dangers of existence might somehow be lessened for yourself with the sudden snatching away of a neighbor or two by predators flashing by, thus lowering the odds of your own demise? Actuarial roulette as a guide to life choices?

The pull against the sardine's desire for independence was of quite a different nature. Aware that the personal ball of whirling disquiet within each member of its species could not be escaped, much like the desperation with which they raced together against death, it acknowledged the cruel reality cast over all their lives like a net no individual effort could break through.

This fate none of them was spared, regardless of how much any one fish might believe it deserved to be exempted. Nor should it be exempted, the sardine conceded. Packed tightly in the bait ball or tightly in a can on a cupboard shelf or "swimming free"—once a sardine always a sardine was a truth that went beyond all independent efforts at self-definition.

Nevertheless, this sense of a fate shared at a distance didn't lessen the loneliness that came at times to a life on the outside. Belonging and self-definition still formed an uneasy balance that neither lasted nor provided much comfort even in the short run. And a return to companionship by default within the bait ball wasn't really a possibility for the sardine at this point, after a lifetime of swimming in larger and larger arcs away from the point where it had set out on its own. Both it and the others had traveled far since then, in directions none could retrace.

That none knew how to retrace.

THE ANT AND THE GRASSHOPPER

Once an ant and a grasshopper crossed paths after being out of touch for years.

They hadn't seen each other since graduating from university together. When they unexpectedly met again, the ant was headed for an important corporate meeting, while the grasshopper was returning from "afar." The ant was wearing a three-piece suit with a company tie clasp. The grasshopper had on a tattered straw hat and generally looked as though it was coming apart at the seams itself.

After their initial surprise had worn off, the two asked each other, almost in unison, "What have you been up to all this time?" The ant told of having been unable for years to find steady employment after earning a degree in Humanities. It had moved from one job to another, without ever feeling secure in any of them. Regardless of its industry and dedication, the ant invariably found its efforts meant little when a business went through restructuring or downsizing. The ant was always among the first to be let go.

The grasshopper, on the other hand, told of a wildly successful career following graduation in Finance. At a time when the markets were posting new highs every session, lucrative investments and bonuses in the millions piled up at such a rate that the grasshopper couldn't spend the money fast enough. Success became an embarrassment and then merely tedious. The grasshopper wearied of its penthouse, its Ferrari and its chauffeured Rolls-Royce, multi-martini lunches, power ties, exclusive club memberships—the lot. One day it sold everything it owned and didn't even bother to collect the profits. Instead, it booked the first available plane ticket to anywhere and vanished.

At about the same time, the ant finally and unexpectedly got the break it had been waiting for. Despondent over its lack of prospects, it had entered a jingle-writing contest for an insurance company on a whim and won. Sensing that it might have found its long-sought road to security at last, the ant threw itself into advancing the interests of its employer and had done quite well, all considered. The mortgage on its house had only another nine years to go, its children were in good schools, and it was contributing faithfully to both a 401(k) plan and an

IRA with an eye to retirement decades in the future.

When the two former classmates finished recounting their tales, they looked one another over with a mixture of bemusement and relief. Each thought of the turn the other's life had taken and said to itself, "There but for the grace of God, go I." The ant wondered what the grasshopper would do when old age came and it realized it had frittered everything away. The grasshopper wondered what the ant had done with the summer of its life.

Following their chance meeting, the ant and the grasshopper went their separate ways and never set eyes on each other again. As it turned out, they both died on the same day years later. The one succumbed to a heart attack at its desk, diligently working away at the sales pitch for a new insurance plan. While the other also died of a heart attack, on the Riviera, surrounded by golden-skinned grasshopper girls.

THE BULL

Once a bull opened a china shop.

That certainly was not by choice. The bull had originally envisioned a career in rare porcelain, the love of its life. It had looked forward to years of dignified connoisseurship, offering the contemplation of superb pieces by appointment and sharing arcane insights with like-minded collectors over cognac. There was not a Sung Dynasty celadon or Ming "blue and white" that the bull could not identify by collection and describe from memory, right down to the cracks.

But it was not to be, this life as an aesthete, spending mornings in a silk robe and later, tailored suits for the auction house. Instead, the bull found itself trapped behind the counter of a small shop stuffed from floor to ceiling with ceramic knickknacks, peddling kitsch to survive.

No circle of venerable cognoscenti passed their time here. Instead, tourists and birthday shoppers squeezed past the shelves of mass-produced figurines and keepsakes. While the bull recited quietly to itself a lecture on Japanese tea bowls that would never be delivered, customers picked up this item or that, turned it over a few times, and then put it back down with a "This one's cute."

The miniature china bulls on key rings were always a favorite. Customers could be counted on to break into nervous giggles, looking back and forth between the tiny figure in their hand and the huge one bent over the cash register as if lost in the machine's enigmas. Out-of-towners were especially prone to buying the key-ring bulls as a memento of their visit. "Who'll believe it when we tell them?" they might whisper to one another as they left the shop with a final glance back.

After the last customer of the day had departed and the bull had locked the door to the shop and pulled the blinds, it would stand motionless awhile and survey the crowded display tables. For those few moments every afternoon, a distant look would come into its eyes.

Then the look would pass. The bull would shrug its broad shoulders and begin walking slowly back down one of the narrow aisles, flicking its tail and randomly knocking a few pieces to the floor.

THE CAT

Once a cat read a newspaper obituary for its just-ended eighth life.

The cat was not pleased. Not pleased at all. It couldn't complain that anything in the obituary was definitely wrong. The dates were accurate, and the facts stated were all true. On the face of it, the obituary might seem a very complete summary of a long and successful life. Nevertheless, the cat was deeply dissatisfied.

"Was that me?" it asked itself.

A life should be more than a list of data, certainly, a bland chronicle of accomplishments patched together from old newspaper files, with a few quotes and a couple of formula sentences inserted at the last moment listing cause and place of death. Where was the life it had really lived, the cat wanted to know as it scanned the obituary again.

Not here, that was certain. What the cat would have observed about itself wasn't even hinted at. Who could guess from this neat tallying up of triumphs that other aspirations than worldly attainment and the attention it brings had ever moved the cat? Or that at some stop along the road to success, it might have regretted any number of detours not taken instead? Who could guess what forfeits and forsakings veiled themselves behind the cat's celebrated stare in the archive photograph accompanying the obituary?

It would be the boilerplate version of a "life meriting praise" that readers took away from the cat's passing, not its own. In place of an individual's chaotic ups and downs, each one a testament to the myriad possibilities of life, they would be given an agreed-upon guide to what every dead notable should have been and should have done. The "official story of the cat's eighth life," but according to whom?

And what of all that the cat had experienced before the first dates listed here? It was as if this accounting of its most recent life had cancelled out every one of the previous seven. They might as well never have happened. Their only virtue seemed to lie in the supposed evidence they provided that one could "start over again" as often as necessary. The cat saw itself turned into a crude, hollow metaphor for self-reinvention: a message to those who'd made good that nothing else mattered and to those who'd fallen short at life that, sorry, but they just didn't have what it took apparently or else hadn't tried hard enough.

At this rate, it might have been better for the cat to be a failure the eighth time around. At least then its life wouldn't have to add up to some pattern that the morning latte-and-obit crowd accepted as the measure of consequence. There would have been room as well for what didn't add up, what would never add up, or wouldn't impress anyone even if it did.

And finally, what was this concluding paragraph about "survived by" meant to say? In what really counted, the cat was survived only by itself. This couldn't be the last thing to set down about it, this presumption that it had been merely a link in some chain of inheriting and passing on whatever the general public felt was important as a legacy.

When it reached the end of the obituary for a second time, the cat didn't even bother to clip it out for saving. Instead, it folded up the newspaper with a dismissive "I was more alive than that!"

THE PHOENIX

Once the phoenix considered having itself embalmed.

Why bother rising from the ashes again and again, it wondered? Why continue as a bright emblem of new beginnings? Nothing much was being made of that opportunity anymore, so far as the phoenix had observed. Those given a chance at a fresh start seemed unable to think of what to do with it except to make out the same wish list they'd made out for their present life.

They wanted power if they'd had none; they wanted to be squillionaires if they'd ever come up short a dime; they wanted to be beautiful and lucky in love if they'd been plain and heartbroken; they wanted to live forever if they'd been sick a single day. If all they hoped for was permission to cancel their disappointments and call it a new life, what purpose was served anymore by going through the flames to show them the way they should have followed?

Was no one longing to be reborn as a person even imagination hadn't breathed life into yet? Was no one longing for a future burned clean of the past, freed not just of failures and regrets but also of recycled desires? Ready at last for anything but a return to what they knew only too well. If not, then a mummified phoenix would be just as good as a live one, wouldn't it?

Certainly better than allowing itself to be cloned, as some suggested, and thus becoming a symbol for the shallow attraction of replaying one's life again and again for the highlights. Still worse would be for the phoenix to bow to the constant urging to retro-engineer its DNA and thus end up standing for the eternal fantasy of never having to grow old and die at all, let alone seek a new start: a once-proud bird reduced to appearing in everlasting infomercials for retirement spas packed with perpetual twentysomethings trying to make sense of experience at three hundred.

If that was the future, a trip to the embalmer definitely seemed most appropriate.

THE SPHINX

Once the Sphinx grew weary of it all.

Who wouldn't, the Sphinx wondered? Waiting here on the approach to Thebes for years to quiz the occasional wanderer who might shamble up (most often lost and in no mood for riddles) had proved more dispiriting than anticipated.

To say nothing of the flies that circled one in this heat, some days so thick they blotted out the sun and so fierce in their assault that the welts they left on the Sphinx by day's end still itched the following morning.

But the wait and the welts could have been ignored if only those who did come along measured up to the Sphinx's wish for the diversion that an engaging test of wits might offer. None ever did measure up. The way they scratched their noggins or other parts of their anatomy and sighed over its riddle for hours on end, missing every opportunity to rework it or expand it or even to ask a few questions in return, and then brought on their doom in an instant with some foolish guess—who should be expected to sit through that?

It was an embarrassment. Spending any time at all with somebody so clueless as to insult one's own intelligence could make the Sphinx want to tear itself to pieces for even having posed its question in the first place. But then to suffer the remorse of dispatching yet another unfortunate clearly not in one's league mentally was worse. After enough of these encounters, how was one to bear the shame of having undone so many of the intellectually defenseless?

Should the Sphinx have dumbed down the riddle so that someone in this puzzled lot might have hit upon the answer? What would be gained, really, by such a move? Wouldn't it cast both the Sphinx and the lucky one in a worse light? The answerer might not have cared, happy just to forestall his or her eventual end, but what of the Sphinx? To have lowered the mental bar and cheapened, right at the start, all that was to follow in a long tradition of confidence in the power of the human mind—was the Sphinx willing to face the scathing contempt such a lapse in judgment was bound to bring over time?

No, better to hold out hope through it all that sooner or later someone would come along who was up to the riddle. Someone who would bring both of them renown by solving it. Like this young man Oedipus here, so full of himself and so sure he knew everything. Was there a chance now at last for a true contest of minds, one that fully deserved to find a place in myth? And yet what did Oedipus really know of life's conundrums that could rival the Sphinx's own awareness? How much didn't he have left to learn about what it ultimately meant to crawl and then stride and then hobble with a cane through the day?

Poor fellow. A greater riddle in himself than any the Sphinx could pose. Yet here they were, trapped face to face in a swarm of flies: Oedipus the Sphinx's best hope for humanity to live up to its claim to wisdom and the Sphinx all that stood between Oedipus and a reckoning no human should have to endure.

Ought it simply spare him that ordeal? Make the riddle one without an answer this time and put a stop to the youth's blind rush towards a terrible fate? Or cry out, "Wait! Give it more thought. You have no idea what any of this truly means."

Or would it be better to stay silent and let Oedipus discover for himself the limits of his understanding? What an agonizing dilemma these questions posed for the Sphinx. At last a wanderer comes along who just might be worth having waited all this while and suffered all these disappointments for, only to put the Sphinx in the position of having to choose between exacting his death if he failed to solve the riddle and its own if he succeeded.

But there was really nothing either of them could do now to escape their plight. The years of the Sphinx's standing vigil here and all of the efforts by Oedipus to flee a dread prophecy had come down to this single moment that held them both in its tight grasp.

As Oedipus finally cleared his throat and began to open his mouth, the Sphinx looked deep into the eyes of the young man and a tear rolled out of one of its own at the knowledge of what the future held.

IX

THE SCORPION

Once a scorpion experienced a moment of compassion.

Compassion isn't a trait often associated with scorpions, either in their own minds or in the mind of anybody having the misfortune to be stung by one. With a secretive, shifty manner plus a tail crooked in a permanent gesture of anger insectified, they have few rivals for instilling fear and projecting a sense of deep-seated malice. Between humans and scorpions, it might almost be said there is a line of mutual loathing that neither has the slightest wish to cross.

Understandably then, feelings of compassion were far from this scorpion's mind early one morning when it saw a huge naked foot swing casually out of the camp cot under which it had been minding its own business all night and descend rapidly towards it. The foot's menacing approach called for a split-second survival response, since if this wasn't already a question of life or death, it soon could be.

From under the arch of its stinger, the scorpion eyed a soft spot on the foot where it meant to plant a venomous strike and repay its own possible end with one equally possible. A life for a life, it was that simple. For why, when one's very existence was at stake, should any life be more valued than another? Was the largest creature granted fuller being than the smallest? Did life flow with anything other than insistent force through all the forms it took? If a human could claim a right to survival, then so too could a scorpion.

As the threatening foot drew closer, the scorpion's entire life flashed before its many eyes. Yet not one of them could identify the whys and wherefores in the scorpion's past that might have led to this precise instant. What in the unfolding of time had brought it to this dreadful pass and to no other? Would the owner of this foot, so unaware and yet equally close to death, also wonder in a second or two what act or decision long forgotten could have begun a journey that would result in horrible agony at this time and this place?

One of them would soon be in no state to wonder further. But what of the other? Living to see another day after so narrow an escape would be welcomed as the better of two outcomes, no doubt. But then what? Another day, and another after that, and after that another, until the undoing barely avoided here arrived without fail in some other way somewhere else?

Granted a temporary reprieve now, what likelihood was there that either one of them would reach old age without suffering anew and often? Heartaches, setbacks, disillusionment, injury, the ravages of disease or despair, the final "sans everything" of physical collapse and mental collapse as well—these were only a portion of what lay ahead. Was this human as keenly aware of what the future might hold as the scorpion suddenly was?

If so, or even half as aware, how could the scorpion not feel a measure of cross-species empathy for a fellow victim of the sorrows that come with the gift of life?

THE RHINOCEROS

Once a rhinoceros noticed it had a bruise.

The mark was only a small one at first, nothing more, really, than a slight mottling of the skin. But how could a rhinoceros come by a bruise at all, that was the question. Few creatures in the animal kingdom had a tougher hide.

Thanks to this toughness, the rhinoceros had taken whatever life threw at it with indifference. Whether exposed on open grassland or hidden by the night, it had followed a path through life few dared cross, and those few only at a trembling scamper. It couldn't recall the last time it had even been snorted at by another creature, let alone actually challenged. Nature's follies did not extend to suicide by rhino, apparently.

So what could have caused the bruise? And why was it spreading? For it was undeniably spreading, at the relentless pace of blood on the move. And spreading in all directions simultaneously. At times the rhinoceros felt such slow but mounting pressure from within that even if its flanks held firm, a simple nosebleed might bring it low.

But its flanks weren't holding firm. Now tender to the touch, they rippled sluggishly as though the rhinoceros was being pushed and scraped around the inside of its own body. At this rate, might it soon be just one enormous bruise, two tons of black and blue on wobbly legs? This couldn't be happening! Not to a rhino in its prime!

A wave of anxiety overtook the rhinoceros at the prospect of such a change from its familiar self-assurance. It had never been known for being particularly light in spirit, of course, but neither had it judged itself to be a glum hypochondriac. Admittedly, there were days when the rhinoceros felt every drop of rain that fell must be falling on its back. Yet its back hadn't given way, and after a short period of listlessness, its spirits had always revived.

Now no longer feeling safe from the worst life could inflict, the rhinoceros realized how close to the skin it had lived for years, unaware. It had grown confident of shielding itself from the world and the worst that life could bring by hardening its senses and stiffening its nerves, and yet there, just out of sight all the while, lay a weakness in wait. A dark vulnerability. Now that it had welled to the surface, what protection was left?

Or was not being safe from bruising actually the price of being alive? The rhinoceros would have to think about that. How prepared was it to suffer whatever might come of allowing the winds and the rain and the heat and all the rest of nature's rule to reach deep within? Welcoming this, however uncertainly, rather than keeping it at bay?

Yes, the rhinoceros would have to think about that.

THE MOLEHILL

Once a molehill came to worry that it might not reach its full potential.

Things had started out well enough in its estimation. Being small was a relative term when all around you, other molehills were just starting out as well. Which of them knew for certain whether it was destined to make a mountain out of itself or not? Which of them didn't have equal scope to shape its future through the power of positive thinking? And didn't all have an equal right, then, to dream of casting long shadows at some point and being looked up to as a monument of molehill success?

Granted, an Everest-amongst-molehills wasn't anywhere to be seen. Instead, in every direction, meager piles of soil rose to about the same level and no further. This didn't mean, however, that in some distant field, a snow-capped peak hadn't thrust itself overnight into the sky as inspiring proof that no molehill should settle for anything less than the realization of its dream. The mere possibility of reaching this goal was enough to temper doubt, even on days when the clouds seemed as far out of reach as ever. In a way, their remoteness gave more room for the future to expand into glittering proofs of achievement.

On warm summer mornings, the molehill would picture to itself the heights it might reach that very afternoon: ever-ascending triumphs that would bring both satisfaction and well-earned recognition. And when afternoon turned into dusk without any of these triumphs having arrived or even hinting they were near, there was always tomorrow to look forward to, with its sustaining promise that would start all over again at dawn.

Nor did those dawns, and there were many, when the molehill thought it might have detected an overnight inching up nearby cause its own confidence to decline. If anything, that confidence grew to fill whatever new gap in comparative stature might seem to have occurred: one molehill's rise could possibly be proof all molehills would have their day in these fields of opportunity as far as the eye could see.

When days stretched into months and months into years, though, and that long-envisioned pinnacle of achievement hadn't materialized, the molehill began to wonder if it was the victim of some unjust meting out of success and failure that ignored the force of ambition. Did other molehills really have more going for them, or did they owe their good fortune simply to being in the right place at the right time?

Such thoughts didn't provide more than temporary solace, the molehill found, and sometimes left it with the sinking apprehension that this inability to reach its envisaged potential might be due to some lack within, an individual deficit that held it from measuring up and making the most of itself. But what could that undermining weakness be? Where in all the abilities it had trusted to lift it when an auspicious moment arrived could so calamitous a shortcoming lie hidden? Or might an assortment of small failings, too trivial to attract notice separately, have combined to deny it the full measure of success reached by others?

These questions repeated themselves over and over, until the molehill had to admit that any answers it came up with simply prompted new doubts and deepening concern. Should it have done this differently or that differently or done nothing whatsoever, trusting in the vagaries of fortune to place it among the high and mighty rather than its own powers?

Other molehills, alone with their thoughts, must also be wrestling with self-doubt and shrinking within themselves at the fear that their most cherished expectations might never be met. There must be millions of similar molehills out there, barely aware of each other previously except as remote challenges to their own personal rise but now gradually understanding their shared reality—one that bestowed no spectacular triumphs, true, yet in its rebuff just might call forth something equal to even the loftiest mountain range. Might there be an unrecognized majesty in their lowly state?

For the greatest of peaks erode with time to less than a molehill, but to find your estimation of yourself thwarted from the start and yet still survive continual defeat, still carry on in spite of it all, must require one of the towering strengths of this world.

THE TOPIARY MENAGERIE

Once topiary animals took the shears to themselves.

At first only a small number dared to snip furtively away at their edges, trimming off a little bit here and a little bit there so the effects wouldn't be noticed by those charged with maintaining the topiary menagerie to standard pruning guidelines. Uncertain of what they were doing, these venturesome few also wanted to guard against getting ahead of themselves and coming to rue the results.

They could have remained as they'd always been, of course. Leaving matters to the experts and their long-established canons of form and proportion would have avoided any untoward missteps. And not a few of the topiary animals themselves nervously warned others against the dangers of redefining their shapes by the slightest degree. Who knew to what lengths headstrong individuals might go in their fumbling boldness, putting the whole of the menagerie at risk of detection and triggering the swift reaction that would assuredly ensue. For topiarists had years of training, and the patterns they followed were time-honored ones. If these were violated and visitors to the menagerie could no longer identify their favorite animals at first glance (or even tell a mouse from an elephant, should things go that far), where would it end?

Such dangers could not be denied, but neither could the frustration experienced daily over the ignoring or outright denial of individual animals' inner yearnings. Shouldn't a mouse have a right, after all, to cherish a vision of itself as a mighty elephant? Or an elephant to harbor an equal hankering to explore the life of the nimble-footed mouse? And any other creature to free the restive psyche within it?

There were bound to be mistakes made as the shears came out in far-flung corners of the menagerie. Many of the animals were feeling their way forward; they'd never before ventured into unexplored territory like this. Sudden liberation of the self could well result in a formless tangle that showed less promise than did the scattered snippets already patterning the ground. Yet boldness might bring inspired sculpting just as often. Who could have guessed that inside a buffalo, a songbird might be awaiting first light or that from a lowly snail a dragon might soar in full majesty? Once such feats of self-fashioning were believed even remotely possible, there was no turning back for the animals in the topiary menagerie.

All became willing to face whatever might await them for this one chance to be seen as everything they conceived themselves to be.

A TREE IN THE FOREST

Once a tree fell in the forest when nobody was there to hear the sound.

The tree had been straight and tall, with a trunk that rose from the ground like a force of nature unto itself, ready to announce its defiance of any lightning strike or landslide. From below, the tree's crown was invisible far above, beyond the many branches that reached through those of neighboring giants on every side, linking one tree to another across ridge after ridge for miles.

Now those branches, shorn away in its fall, spread wide as if to gather up every needle that had ever floated down from them. The broken remains of trees that had toppled long before this one lay here and there around it, their former might now carried away piece after piece by ants.

Surrounded by the deep quiet of the forest floor, the tree began to reflect upon its own state. To have been standing so firmly rooted and now be stretched out here below and within a matter of decades to be no more—these changes might seem a steady undoing of the tree's presence that would end in questions of its ever having existed at all: leaving no more lasting trace of that existence than the sudden thunder of its collapse had left in the air.

Though what difference did it really make whether anybody had heard that thunder, let alone seen the tree's fall? Or that few had even known it was here deep within these woods in the first place? Did what counted about it depend in the slightest on the number of those whose comprehension of such things might begin and end with "Wow, what a big tree!"?

There could be no doubt it had come crashing down, as all trees naturally must. Or doubt that the moss in which it now lay had not been torn and tossed great distances when it struck the ground. And even though new moss would cover its entire length soon enough and reclaim the forest soil when it had finally rotted away, until then its inch-by-inch decline would still bear the shape of a life drawn up over centuries through root and limb and now returning to the earth.

Every ring grown out from the tree's heart had spoken of a force barely held in by now-riven bark that soon would nurse new saplings with its decay. And how many of these would fall in their own time, sooner or later, without the presence of a single witness to what sprouted, matured, and passed away here?

Did any of that even matter? Knowing you'd stood here for your allotted time was enough. As was knowing a forest had stood within you. You, who'd listened to the sound of your fall with the same understanding as when you'd listened to autumn storms rage through your branches or the thawing snow gently drip from them with each return of spring.

You, the sole testimony needed.

Sound or no sound had nothing to do with it.

Witness or no witness had nothing to do with it.

THE TORTOISE

Once a tortoise realized its time was drawing nigh.

The tortoise wasn't particularly alarmed by this realization. It did not suddenly turn morose or self-pitying. Nor was it bothered by those who raced past with an "Outta the way, old-timer!" tossed back over their shoulders. Nor by the likelihood that it cut a figure of ridicule in the eyes of many, what with its sagging flesh and its halting gait. It didn't look upon younger generations with defensive animosity or resentment that its own years were coming to a close while theirs would continue through decades to come. Its life had been full enough for one tortoise.

Thinking back over the years gone by, it took satisfaction not in specific events or experiences so much as in their sum total. What mattered most, now this long life was nearing an end, was that it had included a beginning and a middle as well.

A hackneyed assertion perhaps, the tortoise admitted, but there it was. Grander pronouncements about a lifetime could be left to those who thought them worth voicing. The tortoise was content to know that in its own time on earth, there had been room for challenges and achievements enough. These might not appear all that impressive, no memorable victories gained or harrowing defeats endured, but they would do for a life. They had their own weight and significance.

And despite its having been rather solitary by nature, the tortoise was pleased to have shared the planet for a time with so many other beings. It didn't get out and about much now, but that hadn't always been the case. In its day, the tortoise was to be seen at many a public celebration and cultural event. It seldom missed a museum exhibition or a concert or a boisterous parade or some other public event. And while a night at the theater could carry it to the limits of heart and mind, a walk down broad avenues, surrounded by perfect strangers in an endless flow, could be just as inspiring. Though it personally had always moved at a plodding pace, the tortoise rejoiced that so many others seemed to dance through life with such grace and élan. No question, it was good to have been a participating witness to it all.

Oh, there were countless experiences the tortoise now realized it would never have a chance to embrace. Adventures it would not pursue and longings it would fail to satisfy. But perhaps this was as it should be. To think that all you desired would be granted you in full—what a monotonous existence that must amount to.

The tortoise also knew that when its final hour was up, life's grand pageant would roll on as if it had never existed. It would be forgotten, sooner rather than later, and leave behind only an empty shell gathering dust.

So be it.

THE RETIREE

Once an octogenarian retiree hesitated over the last entry in a crossword puzzle.

Not that there was any doubt in the retiree's mind about what letters to write in the few blank squares remaining. The final clue wasn't particularly challenging by comparison with those for many of the blanks already filled. In fact, the satisfaction normally enjoyed when completing a crossword puzzle faded into a feeling that the end of this one wasn't worthy of the rest of it. It seemed instead to be almost a denial of the many levels of knowledge and experience needed to reach this point.

The octogenarian looked up from the puzzle and around at the tables neatly arranged in the dining hall of the old folks home. Four to a group, the residents sat waiting for their lunch as plates heaped with steaming meat and potatoes were carried out from the kitchen.

What possessed the management to serve up such heavy fare? Did they really suppose an aging stomach could do much more than churn this load around during a long afternoon nap? Or was that the intention in sending the residents tottering back to their rooms like bloated cattle: bed them down for a while so they don't cause any problems until sing-along time with the Activities Director at half past four?

Who among the residents would have believed that all the pledges made to oneself in a lifetime and one's efforts to honor those pledges would come to this? All the commitments, discoveries, and fulfillments that a life involved or should involve, how could they have come down to daily bingo or chair yoga three times a week and loudspeaker warnings about high blood pressure every day?

The octogenarian looked again at the puzzle. The block letters already filling all but the last empty squares had a firm presence that held off the dark spaces bordering them. Yet these lines of neatly arranged letters also suggested a warning. Their steady march across or down the puzzle seemed in its way much like the cruel reduction to little old women and little old men that had trapped the octogenarian's fellow retirees (in disregard of all they might have been and achieved during their lives) here at their tables as strangers to themselves.

Who among them wouldn't long to go back decades and declare,

"This is who I am or hope to be"? But the only escape from their present state now led in time's other direction. Residents vanished from the dining room every week, and yet the management never mentioned their departure, as though any acknowledgement of the reality of death was the one thing the old must be spared. Nonsense. If the people sitting in this room weren't on a first-name basis with the Grim Reaper already, who was? They didn't deserve the silent, squeamish pretense after their disappearance that they'd never really been here at all: that life left nothing of significance to report about them, even their passing.

The octogenarian eyed again the one remaining line of unfilled squares in the crossword puzzle while tapping a pen against lips that spelled out the missing word and then, rather than write it in, looked once more around the room at the other diners and laid the pen down, slowly but firmly.

X

THE GLUTTON FOR LIFE

Once a glutton for Life had a postprandial dream of one day swallowing it all.

Hungry for everything that Life had on offer, the glutton was loath to leave any leftovers. If you weren't prepared to swallow all of Life, he murmured to himself in the dream, what was the point of being alive? In the limited time you're given to lick your chops at will, how much of all you craved could you take in?

And yet how much you must strive to take in, gulping down Life without missing a taste of the smallest morsel! The sweet with the sour, the mouthwatering with the dry as dust, the flaming hot with the icy cold—every enticement to the senses or to fancy—nothing should escape the glutton's voracious appetite. Allowing such a thing to happen would amount to denying a part of oneself. And if the least of Life was ignored or rejected, if any of it failed to be welcomed in full, then Life was incomplete in some measure. And who would be such a fool as to claim Life ever fell short of its own fullness?

From the minuscule to the immense, then, nothing was absent from the glutton's dream. The only worry was waking before all had been savored. If that happened, what excuse could be made? To have the chance of stuffing oneself as full of Life as possible, to best Gargantua and yet overlook a single remaining tidbit, what a failing that would be towards oneself and towards Life!

From the depths of this worry there gradually rose a new one. At first it was no more than a suggestion of self-doubt, the type of shapeless unease that calls attention to itself only by its swirl of shadow within shadow. But eventually the shadows gave way and in their place stood a challenge that seized hold of the glutton's daydream and threatened to reduce it to an idle whim.

How naive the glutton had been! How could even sweat-drenched gorging not fail to prove inadequate? For in order to "swallow it all," would swallowing all of Life be enough? No it wouldn't, the glutton now realized. To swallow all of Life required swallowing as well its converse: Death. It was that simple. Life and Death, Death and Life, each the complement of the other. The glutton was abashed at not having recognized this demand from the start.

All or nothing? Trust yourself to the summoning fullness of your dream or suffer the consequences of its fading away as you awoke to the regret of failing to prove worthy of your own appetites? The time to act was now or never: to stretch your jaws wide as wide could be and bolt down absolutely everything until the veins that stood out on your brow threatened to burst.

"Well," the glutton dreamed on with jaws opening to the full, "here goes!"

THE SPIDER

Once a spider set to creating its last web of the year.

A sudden crispness in the air had alerted it to how little time remained for this most important task. Through the long months of summer, the spider had spun web after web without regarding them as being more than a way to meet its basic needs. But this last one must be different.

This one must be a fitting farewell to web-making itself.

There was no need to snare a final meal now. The spider had thrived on all that chance brought to it each day as it measured the distance between the branches of trees and down narrow cracks in the earth. It had ridden a single thread across the breeze countless times and spread its silken net in the morning dew and the noonday heat and the still of night.

Now something more was required.

Before the spider grew too weak to balance itself any longer in midair, it must draw upon whatever strength and agility remained at its command to fashion a testament to the very art of being a spider.

This final web couldn't be a halfhearted affair. Every web the spider had ever spun, or even attempted to spin, must be remembered in this one. Every inch must catch the spider's last sunrise in sparkling tribute to what had been and what could have been alike. In this record of one spider's end, there must be an echo of all the webs spun by all the spiders in all the mornings of the world.

It must be a web that would make anyone reaching for a stick to sweep it aside pause before something so imbued with the enchantment that comes of weaving together, if only for a time, the bright strands of the universe.

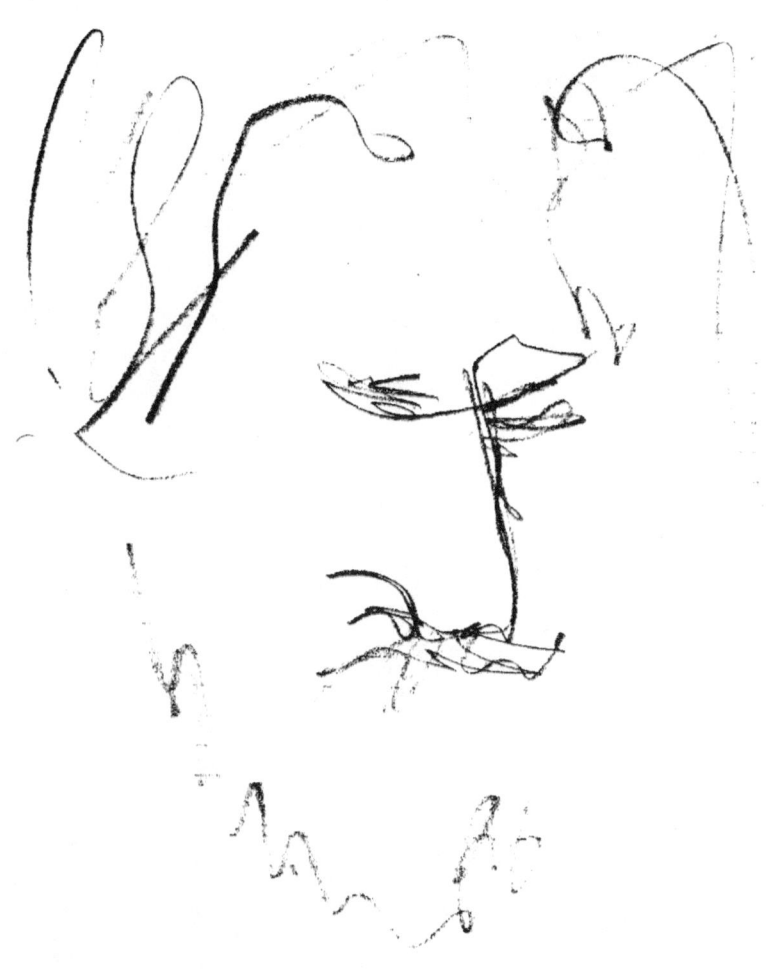

Five-second sketch of the author by J. Spohn